HE'S NOT MY BOYFRIEND

CHIN-WILLIAMS, BOOK 2

JACKIE LAU

First edition: November 2018
ISBN: 978-1-989610-06-0

Editor: Latoya C. Smith, LCS Literary Services

Cover Design: Flirtation Designs

Cover photograph: Depositphotos

[1]

ANY MINUTE NOW, one of Iris Chin's relatives would bring up her single status.

Her oldest cousin on her father's side had just tied the knot. Natalie had had a late-morning ceremony at Toronto City Hall, followed by a multi-course lunch at a restaurant in Chinatown. She and her new husband had headed to their hotel after the reception, and Iris and other members of her family were now at her grandmother's house, which was a short walk from Chinatown.

Iris took a seat in the corner of the ugly brown floral couch her grandmother had owned for decades and waited for someone to mention the fact that she was now the last unmarried grandchild.

Instead, her mother clucked her tongue and said, "I don't know why Natalie got married at City Hall. She should have had a proper ceremony at a church and let her father walk her down the aisle."

Okay, so they were going to complain about Natalie's wedding first. Iris wasn't terribly surprised. Her mother loved to complain.

"Aiyah!" Ngin Ngin, her grandmother, said. "Natalie's married. That's enough for me."

"There's no way Natalie would have gotten married in a church," Seth, Natalie's brother, said with a snort. "And there's no way she would have let anyone walk her down the aisle. You know Natalie."

Mom sighed. "Yes. I know."

There were ten of them in Ngin Ngin's living room, sitting on the couch and on chairs that had been pulled in from the dining room. Iris, Mom, Dad, Ngin Ngin, Uncle Howard, and Uncle Howard's youngest two children, Seth and Rebecca. Seth was accompanied by his husband of ten years, Simon, and their daughter, Livvy. Livvy was a chubby-faced toddler whom Iris had met for the first time this morning. Rebecca was accompanied by her husband, Elliot. The two had wed last year, and Rebecca was now seven months pregnant.

Iris's cousins, unlike her, were mixed race. Uncle Howard had married a white woman forty years ago, and they'd separated last year. His parents hadn't approved of the marriage at the time because they'd been angry his wife wasn't Chinese. But Ngin Ngin had no problem with her grandchildren marrying people of any color now. Natalie's and Rebecca's husbands were white. And Seth had married a man.

Seth handed his daughter to Ngin Ngin, who was sitting on the ugly armchair that matched the couch. Livvy settled in her great-grandmother's lap and poked her chest.

"Pretty," Livvy said.

Ngin Ngin nodded approvingly. "Your daughter has good taste."

Livvy then poked the ugly brown floral chair. "Pretty."

"Um," Iris said. "Seth, does Livvy know any other words?"

"Apparently not today."

Mom clucked her tongue again. She didn't seem to appreciate this line of conversation.

"Livvy, you think Iris is pretty, too?" Ngin Ngin asked, pointing at Iris.

"Pretty!" Livvy shouted gleefully.

"You see?" Ngin Ngin said to Iris. "You're pretty. Livvy says so! No reason you can't find a husband."

Iris looked at her watch. It had taken seven minutes and thirty-two seconds from the time she'd entered her grandmother's house for someone to mention her single status.

Longer than she'd expected.

"I don't think Iris has any problem finding men," Mom said.

"No?" Ngin Ngin said. "Then why haven't I met one?"

Mom looked away.

Iris didn't tell her mother much about her life, but one morning a couple months ago, Mom had stopped by unexpectedly when Iris's one-night stand was eating breakfast with her. Now Mom kept bringing it up, and she made inane comments about how nobody would buy the cow if they could get the milk for free.

But Iris didn't want anyone to buy the cow.

And why on earth did her mother compare her to one? Iris was the *miracle baby*.

Well, that was part of the problem. All of her parents' expectations were heaped on her. She had no siblings to share the load.

Her parents had tried to conceive for the first seven years of their marriage without success. Mom had seen various doctors and Chinese herbalists and despaired that she would never have a baby.

Then, by some miracle, Iris had come along. Mom was convinced it was because of the foul-smelling tea that the fourth Chinese herbalist had made her drink, but Iris had her doubts.

Anyway, Iris was an only child, and she felt like a chronic disappointment, though she tried not to let it get to her. She was happy with her life. She had a good job as a structural engineer, and she went out a lot with her friends. She had sex.

Life was good, aside from the constant judgment of her mother and that pesky issue with her apartment.

"Iris." Ngin Ngin gripped her hand with her bony fingers. "Why is nobody answering my question? I want to know why you haven't brought a nice man to meet me."

"Iris doesn't date nice men," Mom said.

Not only had Mom met one of Iris's one-night stands, but she'd met one who was covered in tattoos and piercings. In fact, he'd been pierced in some rather interesting places.

"What is everyone not telling me?" Ngin Ngin frowned. "Is Iris making the beast with two backs with lots of different men?"

Oh, dear God.

There were some awkward snickers.

"The beast with two backs," Simon repeated. "Where did you learn this?"

"In a movie," Ngin Ngin said. "Did not understand what it meant, so I asked when I went to the community center for English practice. They explained it to me and said it was in a Shakespeare play. *Othello*, I think? Feel very smart now. I quote Shakespeare!"

"Right," Mom said, sounding horrified.

Ngin Ngin turned to Iris. "So? Is this what you're doing?"

"Um…"

"It's okay. I won't judge. You can have fun. I wish I was young again so I could have fun! Not sure about drugs, though. I think drugs are not such a good idea."

Iris just shook her head. Last spring, she'd made a comment about marijuana at Rebecca's wedding. Now her mother and grandmother brought it up all the damn time. If only she could travel back in time and prevent herself from making that stupid comment.

"But you're twenty-seven," Ngin Ngin said. "Still spring chicken, but time to settle down."

"Yes," Mom said. "That's how I feel."

"No making the beast with two backs with everyone. I mentioned Rosetta's grandson before, didn't I? He's nice. I set you up?"

"I don't need you to set me up with anyone," Iris said through clenched teeth. "And I distinctly remember you saying last year that if I was still single in *two* years, you would get to work on matching me up, but it's only been one year."

"Did I say that? I have a terrible memory, and sometimes I say things I don't mean. If you don't want to meet Rosetta's grandson, maybe Mrs. Yee's grandson instead? He's a doctor."

"What kind of doctor?" Mom asked.

"I think it's called a proctologist? Not sure what that is, but it's a big, fancy word."

Being set up with her grandmother's friend's proctologist grandson was just what Iris needed right now.

Not.

"I can do better," Mom said, raising her nose in the air. "You remember Mrs. Yip from church, Iris? Her son is a neurosurgeon. He's just about finished his residency. Poor man. He had a fiancée from med school, but then he caught her making *the beast with two backs* with one of his friends…"

Mr. Neurosurgeon probably had some delightful trust issues.

Iris glanced at her father for help, but he sat silently in his chair, as usual. He was a man of few words and rarely bothered to interfere in any disagreements Iris had with her mother.

This was what Iris didn't understand. Her parents' marriage had never seemed particularly happy to her. Her father was about as talkative as a rock, and her mother was…well, her mother. Talkative enough for the both of them and always sticking her nose into other people's business. They were people who shared a house but had nothing in common.

Then there was Ngin Ngin. Her husband had died nearly twenty years ago. Iris didn't have a lot of memories of her paternal grandfather, Yeh Yeh, but the ones she did have were not fond, and she had the distinct impression that Ngin Ngin was happier without her husband. It sounded like Yeh Yeh hadn't allowed Ngin Ngin much freedom and had discouraged her from learning English, which would have allowed her to be less reliant on him.

Yet Mom and Ngin Ngin were determined that Iris would participate in the institution of marriage, even though their own marriages left a lot to be desired. It made no sense. Iris had no interest in being like her mother or grandmother. In fact, the idea of turning into her mother was positively horrifying.

No, she wanted to remain an independent woman, without a man holding her back in life. She enjoyed sex, but she didn't want anything more with a guy. As far as she could tell, relationships only caused problems and misery.

"So, Iris," her mom said, "which would you prefer? A proctologist"—she made a face—"or a neurosurgeon?"

"I'm quite alright as I am," Iris said. "No matchmaking necessary."

Mom gave her a look. "What's wrong with you?"

Iris adjusted the folds of her blue dress and sighed. "Natalie just got married. Can't we focus on that instead? She's thirty-seven, so I've still got another ten years."

"You can't wait until you're thirty-seven!"

If it were just Iris and her mother, she wouldn't be so restrained right now, but they were surrounded by their extended family.

"How's the apartment search going?" Rebecca asked Iris, attempting to change the topic.

Iris wasn't in the mood to talk about her apartment problems, but it was better than the alternative. "Still haven't found anything."

"What's this?" Mom asked. "I didn't know you were looking for a new apartment."

Yeah, because I try to tell you as little about my life as possible.

"My landlord is kicking me out," Iris said, "because his daughter is moving into the unit."

"How is that legal?" Mom practically shouted in Iris's ear. "You know Mrs. Wong from church—not the one with the mole on her nose, but the one with a bit of a limp, which is because—"

"Mom, I don't need to hear about Mrs. Wong's limp."

"Anyway, Mrs. Wong has a son."

"Of course she does," Iris muttered.

"He's a lawyer, and he can help you sort this whole mess out for free. Why don't I arrange a date—"

"First of all, I am not going on a date with Mrs. Wong's son. Second of all, this is perfectly legal. A landlord can evict a tenant if a family member wants to move in. They have to give you a month's rent as compensation, but yeah, it sucks."

It really did. Iris loved her apartment in Liberty Village. She'd been looking for a new place to live, but it was tough. The vacancy rate in Toronto was low and prices were high.

"I know what the problem is," Ngin Ngin said. "We try to set Iris up with Chinese men, but maybe we should try white men or black men. That's okay with me, Iris. I'm *progressive* now. But Rosetta is Italian. Her grandson isn't Chinese. Why you refuse to meet him?"

"Our new neighbors are from India," Mom said. "They have a son. He's a couple years older than you, and he's a real estate agent. He can help you find a new apartment."

Iris took a deep breath and released it slowly. "For the last time, no matchmaking."

"Just curious," Ngin Ngin said. "You like men of all backgrounds? Anything but Chinese? It seems a bit sad to not like your own people."

"Yes, Iris," Simon said. "What kind of men do you like? I'm very curious."

"I know she likes white men with lots of tattoos and piercings." Mom sniffed.

"How did you gain this knowledge, Carolyn?" Simon asked. "Iris doesn't seem terribly forthcoming on this topic."

Iris sent her cousin's husband an evil look.

Mom looked away. "I came over one morning to drop off some food for Iris, and she had a visitor."

Simon laughed. "Is this true?"

"It's true," Iris said glumly.

"I want to see a picture," Ngin Ngin said. "You have one on your phone?"

"No, I do not. And since you probably won't shut up about it, I have no problems with Chinese men."

"What do you think of Simu Liu on *Kim's Convenience?*" Simon asked. "He's very attractive, isn't he?"

Kim's Convenience was a Canadian sitcom about a Korean family who owned a convenience store in Toronto. It seemed to be fairly successful, and it was unusual for the word "success" to appear in the same sentence as "Canadian television show."

"He's attractive," Iris admitted.

"So I can set you up with Mrs. Yee's proctologist grandson?" Ngin Ngin asked. "Since you do like Chinese men?"

"I have a solution to your problem," Mom said.

"Enough with the matchmaking!" Iris howled in frustration.

"I'm talking about your apartment problem," Mom clarified. "Why don't you move back home?"

"Absolutely not." There was no way Iris was living with her mother again. Plus, she liked living downtown, and her parents lived in Scarborough. She didn't care how much money she'd save. Living with her parents was not an option.

"I have a better idea," Ngin Ngin said. "You can live with me. What do you think?"

Iris shook her head. "No, thanks."

"It's a great idea. Great location."

This was true. The old house that her grandmother had lived in for over fifty years was probably worth a fortune now, since real estate prices in Toronto had skyrocketed and the house was right downtown. Iris would be within walking distance of all sorts of things, and a short distance from the subway.

But no. She was not living with her grandmother.

"I'll cook for you," Ngin Ngin said. "You are a terrible cook, but I can make you all sorts of delicious things. I told you I took a Thai cooking class, as well as learning Italian cooking from Rosetta. Also took Indian cooking class and cake decorating class. Cake decorating is not most useful skill, but it was fun."

Her grandmother was a very good cook, and Iris was terrible in the kitchen. This was true. Still, she was not living with her grandmother.

"You live rent-free," Ngin Ngin said. "Save lots of money and keep me company. Sons say I shouldn't live alone anymore because I'm ninety-one." She glared at Dad and Uncle Howard. "But I don't want to go to seniors' home." Her lip quivered. "What happened to…" She mumbled something in Toisanese that Iris did not understand before switching back to English. "You should respect your elders."

"You can live with us," Dad said, speaking for the first time. "I've told you this before. You don't have to go to a seniors' home, but you should not be living alone."

Ngin Ngin lifted up her arm. "You gave me emergency alert bracelet. That's good enough, no?"

"We're happy to take care of you." Mom was probably not thrilled at the thought of Ngin Ngin living with her but felt she had to say it. They were often at odds, even if they both agreed Iris needed to get a man.

"Not living in Scarborough. This is my home. Have lived here since nineteen sixty-two. Not leaving."

"I put you on a list for a Chinese seniors' home three years ago," Uncle Howard said. "Maybe you will be accepted soon. It's a very nice place. You visited, remember? Much better food than in a regular seniors' home."

Ngin Ngin grunted. "Finally learned to speak English, and now you want to put me in a Chinese home? I have friends here. From all over the world."

"We can still take you to visit them," Mom said.

"No. You will put me in a home and forget about me."

"That won't happen," Uncle Howard said. "I promise."

"Hmm." Mom tilted her head to the side. "Maybe it's not a bad idea, having Iris live here."

"That's what I said!" Ngin Ngin nodded vigorously. "You don't want me to live alone, and I have solution to problem. Iris can live with me and save money. What do you call this? Win-win situation, I think."

Well, living with Ngin Ngin would be better than living with her mother.

God, Iris couldn't believe she was considering this, but she was.

The location. The food. All the money she'd save.

"Please, Iris," Ngin Ngin said. "I have friends, but they're all old. They keep dying. Often feel lonely, but don't want to move. I like my house."

If Iris said no, she'd feel guilty.

She liked her grandmother, though she wasn't so sure about seeing her every day and living by her rules.

As if reading her mind, Ngin Ngin said, "Only one rule. No drugs."

"Alcohol?" Iris asked hopefully. She really needed some right now.

"Alcohol is okay, as long as you don't get drunk. But not marijuana. And you can stay out late. I won't ask questions. You're grown up."

Ngin Ngin wouldn't ask questions?

Yeah, right.

But she probably wouldn't ask as many intrusive questions as Iris's mother.

"If you live with me," Ngin Ngin said, "maybe I will get to meet some of your men with tattoos and piercings?"

"Absolutely not," Iris said, "and for the record, Mom, they don't all look like that."

Mom blanched. "How many…"

Iris sent her mother a dark look.

Ngin Ngin's face brightened. "I can teach you to sew! Will be much fun."

"I have no interest in sewing," Iris said.

"Would offer to teach you to cook, but I'm afraid you're hopeless at cooking. That's why I offer sewing instead. It's mathematical. You will be good at it."

Iris shook her head. "No sewing classes. It's not a necessary skill anymore."

"Okay, okay. But you will be able to change lightbulbs and reach high cupboards."

"You realize I'm only four inches taller than you, don't you?"

"You can stand on a chair or step stool to reach! I'm not allowed to. Your father forbids it. He says I will fall and get hurt."

Dad grunted.

"You will tell me all about your days at work!" Ngin Ngin continued. "I know very little about your job, but I will learn."

"It's really not that interesting," Iris said.

"And all about your friends and who they're dating and marrying. What they name their babies, who's cheating on who, and—"

"My life is not a soap opera."

"Still, more interesting than my life. And we can watch soap operas together!"

"Um… That's not really my thing, and aren't they mostly on when I'm at work?"

"Fine. No soap operas. Maybe you teach me about this thing called Netflick? I hear there are some shows only available on Netflick, but I cannot watch because I don't have it. But we can do it together!" Ngin Ngin beamed. "This will be so much fun. Please?"

Iris would feel very, very guilty if she said no.

"Okay," she said. "When my lease is up in three weeks, I'll move in."

Ngin Ngin struggled to her feet and gave Iris a hug. "You are the best grandchild."

"What about me?" Rebecca patted her stomach. "I'm giving you a great-grandchild."

"If you have twins, then we talk," Ngin Ngin said.

"I've already given you a great-grandchild," Seth said.

"You live in Vancouver. Too far away. Iris is going to do all the cleaning and tuck me in bed and rub my feet—"

"That wasn't part of the deal," Iris protested.

"I tease," Ngin Ngin said. "But I hope you will bring sexy men over to meet me."

"I hope so, too." Simon grinned. "Put the pictures on Instagram."

"Insta—what?" Ngin Ngin frowned. "What is this?"

"It's an app for sharing photos," Iris explained.

"Still don't understand. What is an app? You can teach me once you move in."

"I can't wait," Iris said, unable to muster the appropriate enthusiasm.

Her oldest cousin got to have sex in a fancy hotel right now, while Iris had just agreed to move in with her grandmother. This hardly seemed fair. Plus, she'd spent far too much time listening to her relatives attempt to set her up with proctologists and lawyers.

Though Natalie had put up with quite a bit of that, too, over the years.

Iris excused herself to go to the washroom, then sent a text to her friend Crystal.

Are we still on for tonight? I really need a drink.

Crystal replied immediately. *The wedding was that bad?*

The wedding was fine. My family, on the other hand... Eight o'clock at Elle?

Sounds good.

Excellent. Soon Iris would be able to pour alcohol down her throat and hopefully pick up a man whom she would never, ever introduce to her grandmother.

[2]

IT HAD BEEN a while since Alex Kwong had been out on a Saturday night. At least a month, maybe more. He hadn't planned to go out tonight, either, but then his friend Jamie had called—yes, called, not just texted—and insisted Alex go to a bar with him and his girlfriend.

Frankly, it would probably be good for Alex to get out of the apartment. Have a few drinks, see some people, talk about nothing in particular.

He'd just changed into a polo shirt when there was an unexpected knock on his apartment door. It was his father, carrying a large cardboard box full of food.

Alex shut his eyes for a moment. "Dad, I'm going out tonight."

"That's okay. I won't be here long."

Dad set the box on the kitchen table and started pulling things out. First was some *char siu*—barbecued pork. There was always *char siu*. Then bok choy, green beans, mushrooms, three pomelos...

"They were on sale," Dad explained.

That hadn't needed to be said. If there were three pomelos, of course they'd been on sale, but due to their large size, they were rather awkward for a single person to eat.

And Alex lived alone. As did his father.

Once upon a time, Dad wouldn't have dared to stop by without calling first, and he never would have brought an enormous box of food, but things were different now.

Alex wished they weren't, but they were.

He dug out some small cartons of Vitasoy and a bottle of sesame oil from the box. "You brought me sesame oil last time."

"Did I?" Dad said absently as he removed the last thing from the box: a package of frozen wontons.

"It takes me a while to use up a bottle of sesame oil."

Dad merely grunted.

"What's new?" Alex asked.

Dad shrugged.

Conversations with Dad were often irritating. Alex would try to ask questions, try to keep the conversation going—not something that came naturally to him—and his father would fail to do his part.

Yet he kept coming around with these unnecessary boxes of food.

Once they were finished putting the food away, Alex crossed his arms over his chest and regarded his father. The older man was looking a bit thin, and Alex felt like he should be the one bringing food to his father, not the other way around.

"How's work?" he asked, because he needed to say something.

"Same." Dad shrugged again. "Do you have a date tonight?"

Alex shook his head. "Just going out with friends."

"Right." More silence. "Well, it was good to see you. I'd better be going."

Before Alex could reply, his father was gone.

Well, time to head out to The Thirsty Lumberjack.

∽

Iris and Crystal had started their night at Elle Cocktail Bar, but Iris had the impression it didn't get busy until eleven o'clock or later, and she didn't want to wait around that long. Plus, there was a loud bachelorette party at the front. She could tell it was a bachelorette party because one girl was wearing a flimsy white veil on her head and a black shirt that said "bride" in enormous electric pink letters. The other women in the group were wearing white shirts with pink letters that said "Krissy's Bachelorette Party."

Seemed like a waste to get shirts made just for this occasion. Iris certainly hadn't done that when she'd thrown Rebecca's bachelorette party last year.

Though she'd hired some male strippers.

Crystal Cameron had been at Rebecca's bachelorette party, too. The three of them had hung out all the time when they were at U of T, and they'd lived together in their upper years. Crystal, like Rebecca, had studied electrical engineering, and she'd been the only black woman in electrical engineering in their year. She'd done a master's degree and now worked for a large engineering firm, whereas Rebecca had left engineering entirely and was preparing to be a stay-at-home mom. Rebecca hadn't gone out with them quite as often since she'd met Elliot, especially now that she was pregnant. Iris had invited her tonight, but she'd declined, saying something about making a fish mobile for her baby-to-be.

Iris would definitely prefer to be drinking at a bar than making a fish mobile, but Rebecca couldn't drink right now, and she'd always enjoyed arts and crafts. She'd also said something about "nesting," whatever that was.

"This place isn't doing it for me," Iris said, taking a sip of her fruity cocktail.

Just then, another woman in a white shirt with pink letters ran into the bar and threw her arms around the bride-to-be, and they both squealed and jumped up and down.

How on earth were these people old enough to get married?

Yeah, definitely not the vibe Iris had been hoping for tonight.

"I agree," Crystal said. "Not enough men."

"Definitely not enough men."

There were a small number of men in the bar, but they all seemed to be on dates. Probably not dates arranged by their mothers or grandmothers. Lucky them.

After being bugged about her single status all afternoon by her family, Iris wanted to take advantage of it by going home with a guy and having meaningless sex. Once she lived with her grandmother, one-night stands would probably be off the table. Ngin Ngin claimed she wouldn't ask questions and Iris could stay out as late as she liked, but Iris had no intention of staying out all night once she moved in with Ngin Ngin.

Why had she agreed to this?

Filial piety. Guilt. Money.

Something like that.

Iris could just imagine the scene if Ngin Ngin woke up at eight in the morning and discovered Iris wasn't in her room. She'd call Iris's father or the police. And obviously Iris wasn't bringing any men to stay over at Ngin Ngin's.

So she was going to have her fun while she could.

"I've got the perfect idea," Crystal said. "The Thirsty Lumberjack on King Street. There will be no shortage of men at a craft beer bar."

"I don't know if they'll be the right sort of men."

"Come on. The bearded lumberjack look has really been doing it for me lately."

"You do realize that being called The Thirsty Lumberjack doesn't guarantee there will be any bearded lumberjack dudes there, don't you?"

"Stop spoiling my fun. There's got to be at least one. We'll go there for a few hours, then maybe head out dancing if nothing suits our needs."

"I bet it'll be full of skinny men in toques rather than strapping mountain men."

"You won't know if you don't try," Crystal said.

This was true. It was worth a try. Definitely better than hearing Krissy and her over-enthusiastic friends squeal every five minutes.

Fifteen minutes later, they were standing at the bar in The Thirsty Lumberjack. Iris felt a little overdressed. She was still wearing the blue dress she'd worn to the wedding. She'd thought about changing, but this dress did amazing things to her boobs, and in the end, she'd just settled for touching up her make-up. Crystal was wearing high black boots, a short skirt, and a cream shirt with sequins, and she also seemed a bit overdressed.

Iris felt rather conspicuous. They weren't dressed right, and practically everyone else here was white. And a beer fan.

Iris was not much of a beer fan, and yet here they were.

She ordered some sort of raspberry beer, which turned out to be surprisingly good, and Crystal went with a gose, whatever that was.

"Try it," Crystal said, handing over her glass. "It's not bad."

Iris had a sip and wrinkled her nose. "It tastes terrible. Like drinking someone's sweat."

"I'd happily lick his sweat." Crystal nodded at a scowling man in the corner. He was wearing jeans and a red flannel shirt, and he had a bushy beard that was somewhat reminiscent of the dwarves in *Lord of the Rings*. "He's the perfect lumbersexual."

"'Lumbersexual' isn't a thing," Iris said. "You just made that up."

"I swear! I didn't." Crystal pulled out her phone to prove it.

Okay, fine. It was a thing.

But it wasn't what Iris was in the mood for tonight.

～

Alex looked around The Thirsty Lumberjack. The name seemed apt, given the bar was full of hipsters with beards wearing flannel shirts, though most of them probably weren't fit enough to do any serious wood chopping. A few were wearing toques, even though it was summer.

Alex shook his head in disgust. He didn't approve of men wearing scarves and toques just for appearances.

He sighed and got a table at the back. Since Jamie wasn't here yet, he perused the list of beers on the chalkboard, but nothing really caught his interest. He hated IPAs and sours, and why on earth was gose a thing now?

What the hell was he doing here?

He read through the list again and settled on an oatmeal stout. When the waitress came around, he placed his order.

His dad's visit had put him in a bad mood, and he felt guilty about that. It was a ten-minute surprise visit from his father with an unnecessary box of food. No big deal.

But things didn't feel quite right between them anymore.

The waitress came back with his beer, and he sipped it as he waited for Jamie and Eve. Indie rock music was playing, but it was mostly drowned out by all the loud conversations around him—the acoustics in this place were crap. The table behind him was having a loud conversation about movies, and he wanted to yell at them. Instead, he clenched his jaw and said nothing. He looked around for a TV, hoping to watch a baseball game, but unfortunately, this seemed to be one of those pretentious beer bars that thought it was too good for a television.

Wait—he'd been wrong about that. There was a television in the corner, but it was playing an old black-and-white movie. No subtitles, though. What was the point of that? He wouldn't be able to follow the story. Perhaps he'd check some baseball scores on his phone instead.

"Alex!"

Good. He wouldn't need to sit here alone anymore.

Jamie gave him a hearty slap on the back before sitting down across from him. Eve sat next to Jamie.

Jamie Tsang was a friend of Alex's from high school. He almost always wore a cheerful smile, and he was almost always late. He worked in IT. Eve Appleton was his girlfriend of six months. She had blonde hair and blue eyes and, in Alex's opinion, a slightly annoying laugh, but he tried not to hold that against her because she really was a nice person. She'd even managed to do what Alex had thought impossible, which was to get Jamie talking about kids and marriage and settling down. They'd moved in together a few weeks ago.

"How's it going?" Jamie asked.

Alex shrugged. "Same old. My dad stopped by today with more food."

"How *is* he?" Eve asked.

"I don't know. Okay, I guess."

"And you?" She smiled at him and reached over to touch his hand.

He supposed he liked that she asked him. Nobody else did, now that it had been eight months, but he never knew how to respond. He couldn't put it into words.

"I don't want to talk about it," he said. It was simpler that way.

His mom was dead, and he was going along with life because there was nothing else to do. She'd had cancer, and the prognosis hadn't been good…and four months later, she was gone. Now it was just Dad, Alex, and his younger brother, Stuart, who lived in Calgary.

It was all wrong, but it was life.

He went to work like he always did, he went to the gym every day, he ate dinner in front of the television. He saw his friends on occasion.

He glanced at his watch. One year ago today, he'd learned that his mother was almost certainly going to die.

Jamie and Eve looked at the blackboard with the list of beers.

"What's gose?" Eve asked.

"It's pronounced goes-uh," Alex said, "and it tastes like shit. Like sour, salty water with a bad aftertaste."

"He's not to be trusted," Jamie said. "He doesn't like IPAs."

"I wouldn't mind so much if there weren't so damn many of them. Look at the menu. One porter, and seven IPAs."

"What are you drinking?" Eve nodded at his beer.

"Oatmeal stout." Alex slid it across the table, and Eve tried it and made a face, which Jamie seemed to think was adorable.

Jamie ordered an IPA—of course he did—and Eve ordered a cider. When she circled her hand around her glass, Alex immediately saw the ring.

"You're engaged?" he asked.

She tucked a lock of hair behind her ear. "We are."

"Congratulations." Alex meant it, he really did, though he suspected his tone of voice didn't exactly express that. "When were you going to tell me?"

Eve turned to Jamie. "I told you he'd notice." She turned back to Alex. "My *fiancé* was convinced you wouldn't notice the ring, so we agreed to give you half an hour to see who was right."

Alex stood up and hugged Jamie, then Eve, but he felt a little robotic as he did it. He sat back down and had a long sip of his beer and tried to remember what the right thing to say in this situation was.

"Have you set a date?" he finally asked.

Eve shook her head. "Hopefully next summer, but we have a lot to figure out."

"Right," Alex said. "I bet Jamie wants to get married at sunset under a great white tent, surrounded by thousands of tropical flowers and twinkling fairy lights."

Eve gripped Jamie's arm. "Alex has the best ideas, doesn't he? We should do that. I'll ride in on a pony! What other ideas do you have, Alex?"

"Um. A unicorn?"

"If Eve can find a real unicorn, it can participate in the ceremony," Jamie said, "but people in costume do *not* count. Nor do stuffed animals. Or ponies with horns taped to their heads."

"While we're on the topic," Eve said, "I found a great store on Queen Street the other day. Everything it sells is unicorn- or rainbow-themed."

And that was how a night out with his friends turned into a twenty-minute discussion about rainbows and unicorns. Alex had very little to contribute. He sipped his beer and looked around the bar, wondering what black-and-white movie was playing on the television and why they couldn't show a baseball game instead.

"Do you think he's mad at us for talking about unicorns?" Eve asked in a not-so-hushed voice.

"I assume so," Jamie said, "and, frankly, I've said everything I can on the topic."

"All you did was repeat the word 'no' a lot."

"I'm glad you were listening. Hey, Alex."

He turned his head. "What?"

"You know what you need?" Jamie asked, then gave him no chance to answer the question. "A woman."

"Yes!" Eve said excitedly. "We're going to find you a woman tonight!"

"What is this woman for?" Alex asked. "To marry? To date? Or for a one-night stand?"

Eve shrugged. "Any of the above."

"You can't predict what will happen," Jamie said, then kissed his fiancée on the lips.

Those lovebirds really ought to get a room.

"What about the hipster girl at the back?" Eve nodded toward a brunette with large glasses and a toque. Her beverage was bright red.

"No," Alex said. "I'm not interested in anyone who wears a

winter hat indoors in the summer and who's drinking something that looks like liquid Jolly Ranchers."

Eve rolled her eyes. "The woman with the pixie cut?"

"What the hell is a pixie cut?"

"The woman in the brown dress."

She was decent-looking, and it looked like she was drinking the same thing as he was…and she was now kissing another man.

Okay. That was a no.

He couldn't say he was terribly disappointed. He wasn't in the mood for this, to be honest. Too complicated. Too much effort.

Eve looked over at him. "You've sure been working out a lot lately."

"Shh," Jamie said. "You're not supposed to pay attention to any man but me, babe."

"Aww, jealous, are you?" She slid into the seat next to Alex. "Can I see your abs? Do you have a six-pack? An eight-pack?"

"Um…"

She was right, though. He'd been working out a lot. Sometimes twice a day on the weekend. It felt good to push his body these days, even more so than usual.

Eve wrapped her hand around his bicep. "Flex for me."

He did as requested, though he felt a little ridiculous.

And that was when he saw her. An Asian woman, perhaps Chinese, at the far end of the bar, with black hair and a dark blue dress that ended around her knees. She was laughing at something her friend had said, and she put her whole body into the laugh, and it was just fucking gorgeous. She had an expressive face and pink lips he yearned to kiss.

Her.

Yes, her.

He didn't want a date. He didn't want a relationship. He didn't want any complications.

He just wanted her for tonight.

[3]

Usually, Iris would assume that any man flexing his muscles in a craft beer bar, of all places, was a complete douchenozzle. But this man was scowling—though it was a sexier scowl than that of the lumbersexual in the corner—and it looked like he wanted this to be over.

And then Iris noticed the blonde woman with her arm wrapped around his bicep.

Shit.

Iris's gaze collided with his for a blindingly intense moment.

She looked away. He might be as hot as Simu Liu, but it appeared he already had a girl.

"You want to come with me?" Crystal asked. "Looks like Mr. Lumbersexual has a friend."

He did indeed. His friend looked like a mini version of him, about a foot shorter and without the bulk. His beard was just as big, however, and it looked large enough for a robin or two to build a nest in it without him noticing. That beard kind of scared Iris, to be honest.

Plus, she had her eye on someone else.

But he was taken.

"Sure," she said with a sigh. "I'll go."

"Mm." Crystal batted her eyelashes. "Or maybe you won't."

Iris spun around and came face-to-face with *him*. The Asian man with the great biceps.

He was a few inches taller than her when she was wearing heels, which put him at about five-eight. Overall, he seemed... compact. Lots of muscle and intensity packed into a not-huge—but far from tiny—package. He had a nice tan, which she suspected was from working outside, and short black hair.

"I'll see you," Crystal said, smirking.

Iris was still staring at the man in front of her, but she registered her friend moving toward Mr. Lumbersexual at the back.

She needed to look less like an open-mouthed idiot. Yes. That would be a good start.

"I'm Alex," he said, offering her a small smile.

"Out of curiosity, Alex, who's the woman who was feeling up your arm muscles?"

"That's Eve. She's engaged to my friend Jamie."

Iris followed his gaze to the table where he'd been seated. The blonde woman waved at them enthusiastically, then cupped her hands over her mouth and attempted to shout something across the loud bar, but Iris couldn't make out the words. Possibly it was, "He's single," possibly something else.

"Your friend doesn't mind when she touches you like that?" Iris asked.

"Oh, I think he minded. Just a little. Particularly when she asked to see my six-pack."

"Does such a thing exist?"

"Wouldn't you like to know." He had a sip of his beer and raised his eyebrows over the rim of the glass. "What's your name?"

"Iris. Now that you know my name, can you do for me what you did for Eve?"

He bent his elbow and raised his arm, and she wrapped her

hand around his warm skin. When his muscles hardened, parts of her did the opposite and seemed to liquefy.

Nice. Very nice.

"Iris? I feel a little silly standing like this in a bar. Maybe you could let go—for now?"

She dropped her hand.

"I'd offer to buy you a drink," he said, nodding at her glass, "but you still have three-quarters of a glass to go. What on earth *is* that shit? It looks like melted lollipops or Jolly Ranchers."

"It's raspberry beer," she said, pretending to be affronted. "It's actually quite tasty."

He held out his hand, and she passed him her glass. He took a sip, and she watched his Adam's apple bob as he swallowed.

"That's not beer," he said. "It's alcoholic juice."

"That's why it's so delicious. It doesn't actually taste like beer."

"Then it shouldn't be called beer."

"Don't look at me. I didn't make the rules."

A group of men came in, and Alex had to press closer to her as they walked past to a table at the back. His closeness was intoxicating. His hand landed on her shoulder, and he kept his gaze on hers. When she nodded, indicating that it was okay—more than okay, actually—he flicked the strap of her dress with his finger.

"I like your dress," he said.

"I was at my cousin's wedding earlier, and I didn't bother getting changed afterward."

"You went to a wedding today, and *then* you went to a bar?"

"It was a morning wedding, afternoon reception. There wasn't much alcohol—only a small amount of champagne and wine—and I desperately needed a drink after spending hours and hours with my family." She had a gulp of her alcoholic juice to emphasize the point.

"What's wrong with your family?" he inquired, his hand still on her shoulder.

"I'm an only child and the last single grandchild. I'm sure you can imagine. Everyone is desperate to marry me off, despite my protests. And I've somehow agreed to move in with my grandmother, so there's that, too. But don't worry, I'm not drunk. This is only my second drink, and I plan to stop after this one, so you won't get a chance to buy me a beer."

He slid his fingers down her arm to her hand. "I hope you're not saying you aren't interested."

She inhaled sharply at his touch, at the deep richness of his voice. "I'm not saying anything of the sort."

He twisted the iron ring on her pinky finger. "What kind of engineer are you?"

Ah. He knew what the ring meant. She looked to see if he had a similar ring. He didn't.

"Alex, I don't think you give a shit about what kind of engineer I am, do you?"

She'd done too much talking today. Spent too much time telling people that she didn't want to go out with proctologists and lawyers and the sons of women her mother knew from church. She didn't want to talk anymore. Alex was hot, and her skin sizzled when he touched her...and her instincts told her she was safe with him. It wasn't like she'd just walked up to him and kissed him; they'd talked a bit. Gotten to know each other.

Well, she didn't know much about him except for his opinions on beer and her dress, but that was okay. She didn't need anything more.

"Or maybe you *do* care about what kind of engineer I am," she continued when he didn't answer. "Maybe you want to get my number and go on a proper date and all that before you kiss me. Maybe you want to be engaged like your friend, and you don't know where else to meet women other than a craft beer bar."

"I assure you, that's not the case."

He reached for her other hand and trailed his fingers from the back of her hand up to her shoulder. When he leaned forward, she felt his breath on her cheek for a moment before he pressed a kiss to her lips. Just one press of his mouth against hers. Nothing more. He held her gaze afterward.

"I want to take you home with me," he whispered, dipping his head to her ear. "I want to take you to my bed and use you to forget…and I want you to use me, too. If you just like me for my biceps and my six-pack—"

"So you *do* have one."

He lifted a shoulder. "You'll find out soon enough. And if you like the way I look and fuck—and I'm quite sure you'll like the way I fuck—"

"Cocky."

But she was pretty sure he spoke the truth.

It was progressing quickly. They'd only just met each other, but he was already talking about fucking. There was no pretense that this was about anything else.

She liked it. No reason to draw out the game when you knew exactly what you wanted.

He kissed her again, and she immediately tangled her tongue with his. He cupped her ass and pressed her tight against him, and she could feel his arousal against her stomach. His hand skimmed her side, grazing her covered breast, and she released a soft moan.

They were in a crowded bar, but it felt like they were in their own little world.

It was exactly what she needed tonight. To be lost in physical sensations, enjoying his body against hers, so that nothing else mattered.

"Come home with me now," he said, his mouth right next to her ear.

"Of course." When she stepped back from him, she was momentarily disoriented but soon found her voice again. "I have to say goodbye to my friend first."

"Me, too."

"I need your name and phone number and address so I can text them to her. Just in case."

"No problem." He supplied the details. Alex Kwong, that was his name. He was still standing so close to her, and she could feel his breath on her face.

Occasionally, men balked when asked to provide their information and insisted that they were good guys, but Iris was determined to be as safe as she could when it came to her sexual escapades.

She sent the text to Crystal, then went to say goodbye to her friend, her cheeks warm and her heart pumping in anticipation. Crystal and Mr. Lumbersexual were cozied up at a table, their heads bent together.

"I'm leaving now," Iris said, "if that's okay with you. I sent you his information."

Crystal jolted, as though she'd been off in her own little world and was caught off-guard by Iris's voice.

Iris knew what that was like.

"Okay," Crystal said. "Have fun."

"Don't worry, I will."

She was pretty confident Alex could give her exactly what she needed.

"I'm heading out now," Alex said.

If he'd only been hanging out with Jamie, he would have felt guilty, but Jamie was with his girlfriend—no, his *fiancée*—and Alex had felt like a third wheel anyway.

"Sure thing, man." Jamie winked at him.

"You can bring her to our wedding!" Eve squealed.

Right. He doubted he'd see Iris again after this weekend.

He met her outside the bar. They hailed a cab and headed to his apartment in the Annex. It wasn't far, thankfully, and they soon arrived at the large Victorian house where he lived.

"This is your house?" Iris asked. "I didn't think I cared about your job, but now, I'm curious."

He chuckled. "It was split into apartments years ago."

He paid the cab driver and helped her out of the car and up the stairs to his second-floor apartment. Once they were inside, they looked at each other for one long, tense second, and then they were kissing. He pressed her against the door and held her arms out to her sides, pinning her as he explored her with his mouth. Biting her bottom lip, teasing her tongue... When he slid his mouth down to her neck, she arched against him and moaned.

Fuck, he wanted her.

Parts of him had become dulled...detached...over the past year. Most of the time, that was necessary and good, but it was nice to know he could still physically crave a woman.

There had been two other one-night stands in the past year, and they'd been satisfactory. However, he hadn't ached for those women the way he ached for Iris.

He pushed the thin straps of her dress off her shoulders, then undid the catch on her strapless bra and tossed it on the floor. He covered her bare breasts with his hands, squeezing and running his thumbs over the brown tips, which made her arch against him. As he continued to manhandle her breasts, he brought his mouth down to hers and kissed her. She seemed wilder now, less in control of how she kissed than she had before.

When he picked her up, she wrapped her legs—her feet still clad in strappy silver heels—around him as he walked to the couch. He sat down with her straddling him, his erection pressing against her thigh, and she immediately reached for his shirt and pulled it over his head.

"I've been wanting to do this all night," she murmured, scraping her purple fingernails over his pecs, then down his abs.

He sucked in a breath as she continued to touch him, looking at him in wonder. His cock hardened further and pressed uncomfortably against the zipper on his jeans.

As if knowing that, she undid his pants and pulled his erection out through the slit in his boxers. He hissed as she wrapped her hand around him, aching to be inside her.

"Condom," he croaked, and she pulled one out of her clutch and rolled it on.

It wasn't going to be a leisurely fuck.

Not the first time, anyway.

She raised her hips. He slipped his hand between her legs and pushed the crotch of her lacy panties to one side. He thrust two fingers inside her, preparing her for his invasion, but she was already so, so wet.

"Fuck," he muttered.

She jerked her head. "Now, Alex."

He notched his cock against her entrance, and she slowly sank down on him, until he was completely surrounded by her warmth. She wrapped her arms around his back, pressing her bare chest and tits against his skin, and then she started to move up and down.

He was lost in her. She felt even more amazing than he could have imagined. He cupped her cheeks in his hands as he thrust his hips upward to meet her, and he looked into her eyes, dark with need. Her skin was flushed, her pretty lips parted slightly, and she looked so damn beautiful as she was riding his cock.

Alex moved his hands to her ass and used them to control her movements, thrusting harder and quicker until she clutched his shoulders and called out his name.

After her orgasm, her body was limp against his, though her hands still gripped him for dear life. Without coming out of her, he maneuvered them so she was lying on her back on the couch and he was above her. He pressed kisses to her neck and shoulders and stayed still inside of her.

"Use me," she said. "I know that's what you want."

He didn't need any encouragement.

He thrust into her frantically until he came, growling, his mouth pressed to the crook of her neck, and it was the best he'd felt in a long, long time.

"I hate to trouble you." Iris stood up on shaky legs and pulled up the straps on her dress. She didn't bother with her bra, not now.

"But I haven't eaten since the wedding reception, and I need some sustenance if we're going to do that again."

And she definitely wanted to do it again.

The sex on the couch had taken the edge off, but it wasn't enough. She wanted—needed—more of Alex.

He disposed of the condom and buttoned up his pants, but fortunately, did not bother putting on a shirt.

He was *gorgeous* without a shirt.

"What would you like?" he asked. "My dad stopped by with a big box of food earlier." He lifted up a package of rice crackers in one hand and a pomelo in the other.

She sauntered over to him and dragged her fingernails over his chest before plucking the rice crackers out of his hand and opening the package. She stuffed one into her mouth, like the sophisticated girl she was, and he helped himself to a couple, with slightly less enthusiasm than her, before leading her back to the couch.

When she had a one-night stand, sometimes the moments when they weren't fucking were weird, but even though she barely knew Alex, it felt comfortable to eat rice crackers on the couch where they'd just had sex. She glanced around the room for some evidence of who he was, and her gaze landed on a family picture on an end table. Alex with his parents and brother, presumably. She could see the resemblance between him and his brother in the shapes of their faces.

She looked away and helped herself to some more rice crackers.

It was weird to think of Alex having an ordinary life, when in her life, he was just a sex partner for the night. She'd let him do intimate things to her, let him inside her body, but it was all physical.

Yet he had a job and a family and things she would never know about.

Iris Chin did not have boyfriends, much to the disappointment of certain members of her family, but for a moment, she wondered what it would be like to have more than a short-lived physical relationship with a man. With Alex. To know more about him.

She shook her head. She didn't want that. Her life was great as it was. Certainly better than what her mother and grandmother had had at her age, and she had no plans to change it.

She climbed onto Alex's lap and rubbed herself against his growing arousal.

Good. He would be ready to go again soon.

"This time," he growled, standing up with her in his arms, "we're going to the bedroom, and I'm going to see you naked."

As soon as he set her down on the bed, she pulled her dress over her head and tossed it on a chair. Next, she slipped off her heels, followed by her red underwear, and lay down on her back.

Alex stood at the end of the bed, his arms crossed over his naked chest, and raked his gaze over her body. Her skin prickled and her nipples tightened. She propped herself up on her elbows and spread her legs.

"You like?" she said. She wasn't shy.

He climbed on the bed and crawled toward her, looking predatory.

"I do," he said before claiming her mouth.

His hand slipped between her legs, and he groaned when he found she was wet for him.

How could she not be? He was so damn hot.

He circled his finger around her entrance before plunging inside. He added another finger and thrust in and out of her, setting a steady pace. She continued to kiss him back, but her kisses were sloppy and slow because she was distracted by what he was doing between her legs.

When he pressed his thumb to her clit, she practically jumped.

"Can you come for me like this?" he asked.

She nodded helplessly, and a moment later, she was shattering in his arms, shaking beneath him.

He rolled away from her. She missed his warmth, but he was removing his jeans and boxers, and soon he was lying naked beside her, lazily pumping his cock in his hand. She couldn't look away. He was perhaps average length—she'd seen many dicks in her time—but a little thicker than average, and God, it was fucking hot when he touched himself.

She wanted to put her mouth on him.

She bent over and wrapped her lips around the head of his cock, then sucked him in further. That elicited a groan. She kept on sucking him, swirling her tongue around the head. Later this week, when he jerked himself off, she knew he'd think of her giving him a blowjob.

He pulled her up. "I'm not going to last much longer, and I need to be inside you again."

And then she was on her back, and he was above her, and his sheathed cock pushed inside her once more, making her gasp.

"You like the way I fuck, don't you?" he said with a little half-smirk as he pumped himself inside her.

"I do," she said on another gasp.

"I knew you would."

"Cocky."

His hard chest pressed against hers, squashing her breasts, and she loved being under him, filled by him. When he pulled out, she moaned in frustration, but then he positioned her on her hands and knees, and he was inside her again. One hand grabbed her ass, and the other slipped between her legs and fingered her clit. The sensations were overwhelming.

So overwhelming.

She was flying higher and higher, then tipping over the edge. He thrust furiously and came at the same time, collapsing on top of her.

~

When Iris woke up at six the next morning, there was an arm wrapped around her.

Huh?

She and Alex had been on opposite sides of the bed when they'd gone to sleep last night, no physical contact. Cuddling wasn't her thing. But now, a strong male arm—God she really did love his arms—was draped over her hip.

She couldn't say she minded. It felt nice. Solid. Comforting.

Iris immediately jumped out of bed.

She did not need a man to give her any of those things. She was an independent woman, and she did not depend on anyone.

Didn't depend on men to give her orgasms—she could do that herself. Although it was always nicer when she came from a man's cock and fingers and tongue. Particularly Alex's.

Last night had been exactly what she needed.

But she didn't want to wait around until he woke up—who knew when that would be, and the morning after was always awkward. If she woke up early, she usually just left, and this morning would be no exception.

Even if another round of sex sounded awfully appealing.

Yeah, she could admit that it had been a better-than-average one-night stand, but she wouldn't let herself dwell on it now that it was over.

She pulled on her underwear and bra, which she found near the front door, and the dress she'd worn to Natalie's wedding. Her shoes seemed too high and glittery for six o'clock in the morning, but whatever. She put them on. Then she took one last look at Alex. He lay in bed with his arm curled behind his head. The sheet was pushed down to his hips and she admired him for a moment before quietly closing the door and leaving.

She'd never see him again, and she ignored the slight pang in her chest at the thought.

This was the life she wanted, wasn't it?

$\sim$

When Alex woke up, he was alone, which was a normal occurrence.

Except he hadn't been alone when he'd gone to sleep last night. There had been a woman curled up on the other side of the bed.

Iris.

He jumped up and hurried through the apartment looking for her, but she was nowhere to be found. Her clothes and her purse were gone.

She'd left without saying goodbye.

Women never did that to him.

Dammit, he'd been looking forward to having one last round with her before she headed into the sunshine. Maybe even asking for her number so they could meet up again next weekend.

Not for a date. Just for another night in bed.

He went into the washroom to see if she'd written her phone number in lipstick on the mirror, but of course she hadn't. That was a silly thought.

She had his number, though he had a feeling she wouldn't use it.

He showered to wash the scent of her off his skin, and then he got dressed and started peeling a pomelo for breakfast. The skin of the citrus fruit was thick, and the bitter membranes on the individual pieces had to come off, too. He ate half the pomelo and a bowl of cereal, and to his frustration, he thought of Iris the whole time. The curve of her ass, the curve of her breast. Her slick heat as he slid his fingers inside her. Her mouth on his cock —that had nearly undone him.

Fuck. Why had she left?

He shouldn't be angry. It had been all about sex; it didn't mean anything, and she'd made no promises to stick around the next morning. Yes, it had felt amazing to be inside her, but he hardly knew her, even if he knew the sounds she made when she came.

His phone vibrated. A text message from Jamie.

How was your night?

Strange that Jamie was texting him first thing in the morning. His friend usually slept until ten or eleven.

Alex looked at the time on his phone. Holy shit. It was after ten. He never slept this late. He had to wake up early for work, and he rarely slept in past seven or eight on the weekend.

Good, he replied, not in the mood for this conversation.

Well, it *had* been good, even if he was in a pissy mood now. It had been exactly the distraction he'd needed, and now he would return to his regularly-scheduled life and try to forget about Iris...whatever-her-last-name-was. He didn't even know.

Maybe he'd start by cleaning out his freezer, which was packed to the gills now that his father had started bringing him food all the time. He'd go through his cupboards, too. Do a load of laundry. In the afternoon, he'd run some errands and go to the gym.

But he was certain that no matter what he did, he wouldn't get Iris out of his mind.

[5]

THIS WAS the end of life as Iris Chin knew it.

She carried her desk chair up to her new bedroom on the third floor of Ngin Ngin's house. On the way down the creaky stairs, she encountered her father, who was carrying up a box of clothes.

It was the Saturday before the lease on her Liberty Village apartment was up, and she was moving in with her grandmother. Her father had borrowed a friend's van, and he and her mother were helping with the move. Ngin Ngin was supervising. Dad had tried to get his mother to stay on the main floor, but she insisted on going up and down the stairs and just generally getting in the way.

"What's in that box?" Ngin Ngin asked as Iris entered the house. "Why you have so much stuff?"

"Jewelry," Iris said. "Scarves. Purses."

Plus condoms and her small collection of sex toys, but she wasn't going to tell Ngin Ngin about those.

It had been so nice when she'd moved out of her parents' house and no longer had to strategically hide things from her mother. Putting things in a drawer was certainly not enough to keep her mother from finding out about them—oh, no. Her mother was a master snoop.

Iris suspected Ngin Ngin was not as dedicated a snoop as Mom. Still, she might be prone to a bit of snooping, even if Iris's room was on the third floor and Ngin Ngin rarely went up to the third floor anymore. That might change now that Iris was living here.

"This will be so much fun!" Ngin Ngin said as Iris paused on the main floor to have a drink of water. "We're roommates!"

"Yes. So much fun," Iris said, heavy on the sarcasm.

She couldn't help smiling, though. It was nice to see her grandmother so excited.

"You can teach me all the hip new things," Ngin Ngin continued.

"Right."

"We'll listen to the hottest radio stations."

"Nobody listens to the radio anymore."

Ngin Ngin frowned. "Fine. You show me how you listen to music. You show me the latest dance moves, too."

"Um."

"I'm ninety-one but young at heart. I can learn. Who are the hottest heartthrobs these days? You have posters in your room?"

"No, I do not have any posters in my room."

"I like Robert Redford. You know Robert Redford?"

"Isn't he, like, over eighty?" Iris pulled out her phone and looked at his Wikipedia page. "Yes. He's eighty-two."

"Spring chicken! Almost a decade younger than me. I used to like older men, but once you're over ninety, that becomes a problem. Men who are older than me are all dead!"

Iris did not know how to respond to that.

"I used to watch his movies," Ngin Ngin continued. "Did not really understand them because my English was very bad, but I watched for eye candy. That's what you call it, yes? Eye candy?"

"Sure. Eye candy."

"You can find old Robert Redford movies on Netflick for me. Maybe I'll understand them now."

"Okay. We can do that."

"I will buy popcorn for movie nights."

Iris was starting to worry that this move was a very, very bad idea. Would her grandmother expect her to be around every minute she wasn't at work?

"You know I have my own life," she said hesitantly.

"Of course I know! Silly girl. You must go out to meet boys. But I will cook for you during the week and we can have dinner together. On Sunday night, we can watch movies. Sunday night is Ngin Ngin and Iris time." Ngin Ngin wrapped her arm around Iris's waist and squeezed. "Now go finish moving."

Another half an hour, and Iris was finished moving in, more or less. She had some unpacking to do, but all her furniture was in the right place, and all her boxes were in the bedroom. The box with the jewelry and sex toys was under several other boxes —she'd made sure of it. Her couch and her coffee table were in the other third-floor bedroom, though she didn't know if she'd use them much. Her dining room furniture would be stored at her parents' house.

Once the van was empty, she sat at Ngin Ngin's kitchen table with her parents and grandmother, drinking tea.

"Take her grocery shopping once a week," Mom said to Iris. "Make sure she doesn't run out of her meds. Your father and I usually come every two weeks to do some vacuuming and cleaning, but you can do that now."

"Aiyah," Ngin Ngin said. "I can buy food myself in Chinatown. Don't need help."

"You'll need more food now that I'm living here," Iris said. "I'll take you every weekend. If you need to get something small during the week, you can take your cart to Chinatown."

"Don't need help with meds. Easy to manage." Ngin Ngin

shooed Mom and Dad toward the door. "Now go. Iris and I need to draw up roommate agreement!"

A roommate agreement. Seriously?

A half hour later, Iris had written down a list on a sheet of paper.

According to the roommate agreement, Iris would wash all the dishes, and Ngin Ngin would cook all the dinners, except on Saturday, which she proclaimed "date night" for Iris. They would go grocery shopping on Sunday mornings, but not too early, in case Iris had been out late the night before. Iris would do the vacuuming and clean the washrooms. Ngin Ngin offered to do all the laundry, but Iris felt a bit weird about that and planned to renegotiate it tomorrow. Sunday night they would watch a movie, but not too late, because Ngin Ngin got tired early. Sunday afternoons, Ngin Ngin went to Mrs. Yee's to play mah jong.

"I never come back before five," Ngin Ngin said. "So, if you want to have a man over—"

"Please don't finish that sentence," Iris begged.

Alex immediately popped into her mind—he'd done that sporadically over the three weeks since they'd slept together. Iris was starting to resent him for it, even if it wasn't his fault.

No, it *was* his fault for looking so damn hot and being really good in bed.

What would Ngin Ngin think if she met Alex? Would she ask him inappropriate questions, like if he could take off his shirt and flex his bicep for her?

No, that's just what Iris would ask him to do. Not that she was going to see him again, and he was definitely never going to meet Ngin Ngin.

Although Iris *did* have Alex's number, and Ngin Ngin *was* out of the house between one and five every Sunday afternoon…

Tempting, but no.

She didn't want anything that remotely resembled a relationship, and even if she desired more spectacular sex, she'd left his apartment early in the morning, without even saying goodbye or leaving her phone number on a napkin. She doubted he'd want to hear from her again.

Anyway. No more thinking about Alex. She'd focus on her new living arrangement, which hopefully wouldn't be too bad, but only time would tell.

∽

"Wake up. Wake up!"

Iris wasn't used to someone screaming in her ear first thing in the morning. She hoped Ngin Ngin wouldn't do this on a regular basis.

Shit. Maybe Ngin Ngin was screaming because something really *was* wrong.

Iris jolted up. "Is there a fire?"

Ngin Ngin clucked her tongue. "No fire. But it's nine o'clock. You should be up!"

"It's Sunday. I'm allowed to sleep in."

Ngin Ngin furrowed her brow. "You were not out late last night. No reason for you to sleep in so much. Or did you sneak a boy into your room? Is that why you're tired?"

"No, I did not sneak a boy into my room."

Her grandmother pinched the fabric of Iris's oversized white T-shirt. It was well-worn and had holes around the neckline.

"Why you sleep in this? I can teach you to sew. We will make a nice nightgown."

Iris sighed. "It doesn't matter what I wear to bed. I don't need to look nice for anyone."

"Maybe that's why you cannot get a man. You should wear a sexy nightgown, not this." Ngin Ngin made a face.

"So you think I'm having men sleep over on a regular basis?"

"Why not? I know how things work. Everyone has sex before marriage. Am old. Not stupid."

Well, Iris wasn't going to protest and say she'd never had sex.

"I forget why I'm here." Ngin Ngin paused, then raised her finger in the air. "Yes! I remember. You must get out of these rags and come downstairs. Now."

"As you wish," Iris said with a sigh.

She put on jean shorts and a T-shirt, and when she got downstairs, she heard a motor running. The neighbors must be cutting the grass.

Wait a second.

Iris reached the back door in the kitchen, which led to the backyard.

Someone was cutting Ngin Ngin's grass.

In fact, the someone in question was an attractive young black man wearing gym shorts...and nothing else.

"Very handsome, no?" Ngin Ngin said, suddenly appearing at her shoulder. "I told him to take off his shirt. That was my idea."

Iris could do nothing but stare at her grandmother. Usually, Iris was the one who cut Ngin Ngin's grass. She'd come over once a week to do it. It didn't take long, since the backyard was very small, but now Ngin Ngin appeared to have hired a man to do her job—shirtless!—even though Iris had just moved in.

"Did you hire him for the eye candy?" Iris asked. "I don't think it's appropriate to ask people to take off their shirts like that."

"Silly girl. Am not paying him."

Iris looked out the door again, and an awful realization crept over her.

"You're trying to set us up!" she exclaimed. "I told you no matchmaking, and yet I've been here less than twenty-four hours, and you're already doing it."

Ngin Ngin grinned. "Jonathan is the son of Dee, my friend. Dee is from Jamaica, and she and husband run Jamaican restaurant in Kensington Market. I see her every week. Don't understand half of what she says because I struggle with Jamaican accent, but I think she understands everything I say. She wishes for son to settle down and get married, and I wish to find husband for you, so we made a plan! You have love at first sight?"

"No, I do not. That's just bullshit."

"Not bullshit. I have experience."

Iris raised her eyebrows. "That's what happened the first time you saw Yeh Yeh?"

Ngin Ngin waved her hand away from her and turned to look out the door. Jonathan was now trimming the edges of the lawn. He looked up and waved at them.

"Ngin Ngin, you experienced love at first sight with Yeh Yeh?" Iris was intrigued by this. Her grandparents' marriage, from what she'd been able to glean, had been miserable, but perhaps it had been different at the beginning.

"Aiyah. Stop annoying me."

Iris assumed that was a "no." Interesting. Had there been someone else after Yeh Yeh? Before him? Or while she was married?

"No love at first sight...that's okay," Ngin Ngin said. "But you agree he's very attractive, yes? If I was young—"

"I don't think you're supposed to admire men who are sixty years younger than you."

"He's sixty-three years younger than me."

"Right."

"Am old. Not dead. He has nice muscles. You don't agree?"

Iris decided not to answer that question.

Jonathan did, indeed, have a nicely-toned body, and he was handsome. But to her frustration, she found herself comparing him to Alex and finding he came up short.

Not that she would have wanted to go out with Jonathan anyway.

This was the man her grandmother was trying to set her up

with, for God's sake, and she wasn't interested in any attempts to marry her off. She was happily single.

Ngin Ngin clucked her tongue. "I think he's finished now. He's coming inside. You must flutter eyelashes and look pretty. Would be better if you'd brushed your hair."

Jonathan stepped inside and picked up his grey T-shirt, which had been draped over the back of a kitchen chair.

"No!" Ngin Ngin squeaked. "Not yet."

"Let the man put on his shirt." Once he'd done that, Iris stuck out her hand. "Hi. I'm Iris. Sorry my grandmother has involved you in her plan to marry me off. I'm sure you're great, but I'm not interested in anyone at the moment."

"No problem. Neither am I. I just came here this morning because my mother insisted."

"See!" Ngin Ngin said. "He's a keeper! He respects his mother! And he has his own business. Landscaping company." She turned to Jonathan. "At work, do you take off your shirt on very hot days?"

Iris just prayed that Ngin Ngin wouldn't ask if she could come watch.

Fortunately, she didn't.

"Would you like some water?" Iris asked, trying to be polite. "Coffee?"

"Coffee would be great, thank you."

Ngin Ngin decided to give Iris some time alone with Jonathan so they could get to know each other. They talked for twenty minutes and drank coffee, and it was pleasant enough, but nothing more than pleasant.

Once Jonathan left, Ngin Ngin came back downstairs.

"So? Isn't he a great catch?"

Iris was practically pulling out her hair in frustration. "I told you. No matchmaking. Why can't you listen?"

"I listen, but I don't agree. So, I do what I want."

Well, it looked like living with Ngin Ngin wouldn't be so easy after all.

After a not-so-relaxing weekend, Iris was glad to escape to work on Monday morning. She worked at a small structural engineering firm in midtown called Lowry Engineering. Sometimes she took transit to work, but today she drove because she had to go to site in Markham later.

"Hey! How was your weekend?" Emma asked as Iris walked into the office. Emma was the other female engineer at Lowry, and she had the desk next to Iris's. She was ten years older and had been a mentor of sorts.

"I moved in with my grandmother," Iris said.

"Right! How did that go?"

"She's already tried to set me up with someone. She got the son of one of her friends to come over and cut the grass—shirtless—at nine in the morning yesterday."

Emma started laughing.

"She's going to be the death of me," Iris muttered. "Then in the evening, we watched *Barefoot in the Park* on Netflix after I set up the internet. My grandma likes Robert Redford."

Sunday movie night with Ngin Ngin hadn't been too bad, actually. In the afternoon, Iris had had a break from her grandmother —who'd gone to play mah jong—and had done a lot of unpacking. But in the evening, it had been nice to have company, even if Iris had to pause the movie every ten minutes because Ngin Ngin kept asking her questions. Ngin Ngin had also brought out her popcorn maker from the eighties, so they'd had popcorn with melted butter. Probably healthier than the microwavable stuff.

"How was your weekend?" Iris asked Emma.

"Oh, you know. Maddie emptied a bottle of shampoo in the

only room where we have carpet, so that was a mess." Maddie was Emma's two-year-old daughter.

Iris poured herself some coffee and got to work on a report that she had to finish by the end of the day. At ten-thirty, she drove out to Markham. She and Emma had worked on the structural engineering for an addition to East Markham Hospital. Some rich guy had donated a lot of money to the hospital and was having a new cardiology wing named after him. Construction on the addition had started recently, and today they were supposed to pour concrete for the foundation. Iris had to inspect the formwork and rebar first to make sure everything was as it should be. Emma had done the past couple of site visits, but she'd been put on a new project that was taking up a lot of her time, and Iris would now have to come here about once a week.

No big deal. Iris didn't mind going to site on occasion, as long as it didn't take too much time away from her other work. Sometimes it felt a bit strange—she was often the only woman on site —but it was nothing she couldn't handle.

She parked her car and put on her steel-toed boots, her safety vest, and her hard hat. She got out her clipboard with the structural drawings of the addition and headed toward the trailer, where she would sign in and meet the site supervisor, who worked for the general contractor. His name was Alex, but that was all she knew.

Which reminded her of...

No. She wouldn't go there. She needed to stop thinking about *that* Alex. It had only been a one-night stand, and that was three weeks ago now. Time to push him out of her mind.

There were two men standing by the trailer, and they turned toward her as she approached. The man on the right was a tall, middle-aged guy with a crooked smile, and the man on the left was smaller in stature and...

Iris's stomach dropped.

It was *that* Alex after all.

[6]

IRIS COULDN'T BELIEVE IT. The site supervisor for the East Markham Hospital job was Alex Kwong.

This was horrible.

She hated when her personal and professional lives mixed. She took her job seriously, and she would *never* sleep with a co-worker or a contractor.

But now her latest one-night stand had come back to bite her in the ass.

She was going to have to see Alex Kwong every week for the near future, and she'd slept with him, then hurried out of his apartment before he woke up the next morning.

Well, she would remain professional and hoped he'd do the same.

Though given they'd spent the past ten seconds staring at each other without speaking, perhaps they weren't off to the greatest start. Unfortunately, he was just as attractive as she remembered, and she also remembered what he looked like underneath that safety vest and T-shirt…

She pushed that out of her mind.

"Hi," she squeaked. She couldn't seem to say anything else.

He nodded at her. "Hi."

There was a moment of silence.

"Ooh, this feels awkward!" said the man standing beside Alex, clasping his hands together. "You guys sleep together or something?"

Jesus Christ.

"Yes," Alex said in a clipped voice before Iris could respond.

Bastard. Why did he feel the need to say that?

The other man bent over and started laughing.

"Get back to work, Carlos," Alex said.

Carlos gave him a smile and a mock salute before heading off.

Iris waited until he was far away before hissing, "Did you really have to tell him we'd slept together?"

"Nice to see you, too, Iris."

"He's going to tell everyone that you slept with the engineer, isn't he? Fuck. I have a reputation to protect. Maybe it's all well and good for *you* to brag about how we had sex, but think about what it's like for me, okay? I need to maintain my professional integrity, and I don't need these rumors floating around."

Alex looked at her for a moment, and she felt her skin prickle.

Goddammit.

She wasn't immune to him, not by a long shot.

Alex hadn't meant to admit that he'd slept with the engineer from Lowry, but the answer had popped out of his mouth as soon as Carlos had asked the question.

And yet a part of Alex was pissed off that Iris was so angry at him. It rubbed him the wrong way. Consenting adults having sex —it was no big deal.

He crossed his arms over his chest. "I'm sorry I said that. The answer just slipped out."

Iris rolled her eyes. "Yeah, sure it did. You don't sound very sorry. I think you wanted to brag about your sexual conquests."

"Did it sound like I was bragging? It's just instinct for me to answer a question honestly. Normally that serves me well, but this time, I admit it was a mistake."

"This isn't some little mistake. A man sleeps with a woman, his co-workers slap him on the back. A woman sleeps with a man, her co-workers think she's a slut."

"I don't think it's quite that simple, but—"

"Shut up, Alex." Her cheeks were turning red. "You don't know what it's like to be a woman, especially in a male-domi-nated field like this one. I am not ashamed of what I do in my free time, but it has absolutely no place in our work lives. Why couldn't you have pretended you were meeting me for the first time?"

"But I wasn't meeting you for the first time. It would have been weird to ask for your name."

"You could have pretended we'd met before in a professional capacity."

"You know this whole thing could have been avoided if you'd actually told me what kind of engineer you were when I asked."

She would have said she was a structural engineer, and, being familiar with many structural engineering companies because of his job, he would have asked where she worked, and he would have been somewhat prepared for this moment.

Or maybe she would have refused to sleep with him because she worried their work lives might cross at some point. He wasn't sure.

"Well, *sorry*." She put her hand on her hip. "Sorry I wasn't in the mood to talk about my job that night."

It was weird to speak to a woman at work when he knew what sounds she made when she came, and how it felt to push inside her...

Focus.

Instead, he blurted out, "Why the hell did you leave before I woke up?"

"Poor baby. Did I injure your delicate ego? Do you think you're just so amazing in bed that no woman would dare leave without a morning quickie?"

He clenched his fists and stepped forward until he was standing a touch closer to her than would normally be appropriate.

"You enjoyed it," he said, his voice low. "A lot. I promised you'd like the way I fucked, and you did, didn't you?"

"No."

"Liar. Why didn't you stay?"

Three weeks later, it still rankled that she'd left without saying goodbye, though he wasn't sure why he felt that way. It wasn't like he'd planned to take her out on a date. He wasn't interested in anything more than a few rounds in the sack with a woman.

She still hadn't stepped back, even though he was invading her personal space. Her lips were so close. Not bright pink, like they'd been last time, but just as enticing.

Iris on a construction site was as hot as Iris in a fancy dress in a dimly-lit bar.

She finally took a step away from him. "It was six o'clock in the morning, and I was wide awake. I wasn't going to wait around until you woke up."

"You could have woken me up."

"In my experience, most people don't like being shaken awake at six in the morning."

"You didn't need to shake me awake. You could have kissed your way down the muscles you'd admired." He couldn't seem to help it. She was a firecracker, and he liked getting under her skin.

She rolled her eyes. "Fuck you."

"I would quite enjoy that, thank you."

The corners of her mouth quirked up, and then she clenched

her jaw. "Alex, I'm here because I have a job to do, and I'd appreciate it if I could get started. We need to get that concrete poured today, and it can't be done until I give my approval."

"Very well." He set off toward the building in progress. The soil engineer had been here last week and had given the go-ahead. Now they were just waiting on Iris.

They walked around, saying nothing to each other but terse comments related to the job. He could feel the anger vibrating off her.

"The spacing of the rebar is wrong here." She pointed at the rebar in question and then at the corresponding part of the drawing on her clipboard.

"You're just saying that because you're pissed at me."

"Fuck off."

"You really seem to like that word. Just an observation." He stuck his fingers in his belt loops and rocked back on his heels.

"I am a *professional* engineer, and I would not make unnecessary work for you if I didn't need to. How long will it take to fix?"

"Maybe half an hour?" It was just a small area; it wasn't a big enough problem that the concrete pouring would need to be delayed another day, thank God.

"Good. I might as well wait around then, rather than having you send me photos."

They finished walking around the site in tense silence. Luckily, Iris didn't find any other issues.

"I'll be in my car," she said. "Eating lunch and writing a report. Let me know when it's done."

She hurried off, not waiting for a response.

Fucking Alex who made her swear like a sailor.

Fuck. Fuck. Fuck.

She took a deep breath. It would be okay. It wasn't like she had to see him at the office every day. Just a couple hours a week until this project was finished, and then hopefully she'd never have to work with him again. Although her company worked with LBZ on many projects, LBZ was a large general contractor and they had lots of site supervisors. There was a good chance she'd be able to avoid him for a while after this project was done, and if she had to work with him again in a few years, surely he wouldn't have much effect on her.

And surely he wouldn't tell whoever happened to be with him at the time that they'd slept together, unlike this morning.

She still couldn't believe he'd done that.

It just slipped out.

Yeah, sure it did.

Infuriating, attractive man. Who was very good in bed. And on the couch. She bet he was good on any flat surface. Even vertical surfaces, like the door.

Somehow, they'd have to learn to work together. Fortunately, she didn't have to be super friendly with him. All she had to do was walk around the construction site, making sure the work was getting done and telling him what they were doing wrong.

She would rather enjoy doing that.

Although when they were in bed or on his couch, he sure hadn't done anything wrong...

Enough, Iris.

Unfortunately, she was stuck here for the next thirty minutes or so. She turned on the car so she could roll down the windows, then got out her laptop while she waited. She also pulled out the sandwich she'd brought for lunch. Ngin Ngin teased her about her terrible cooking skills, but Iris was at least able to make a damn cheese and ham sandwich and cut up a few carrot sticks, although her grandmother had watched over her while she made her lunch this morning, as if she were a small child who needed supervision while using a knife. Ngin Ngin had seemed surprised when she didn't draw blood.

Iris ate her lunch and worked on her report. Typing on her laptop in the car wasn't terribly comfortable, and a little while later, she turned to open the door, wanting a quick stretch.

"Oh my God!" She jumped in her seat.

Alex's face was right in front of the car window.

"Oh my God," she repeated, pissed off that he'd scared her.

"My apologies," he said through the open window.

"You're probably very pleased with yourself for giving me such a fright."

"No," he murmured, reaching into the car to put his hand on her shoulder, "but I was very pleased with myself three weeks ago when I—"

"Enough. Is there some way I could knock you over the head with a piece of rebar so you'd lose your memory of that night?"

"Threatening violence. How professional of you."

She gave him a dark look.

"It seems awfully cruel to want to give me amnesia," he said. "Amnesia is a very scary thing. On the news the other day, I saw—"

"You idiot. I only want to remove twenty-four hours of your memory. In fact, twelve hours would be more than sufficient."

"It should have been more than twelve hours from the time we met until the time you disappeared, but *somebody* felt the need to sneak off the next morning, and I assure you, it wasn't me."

"Enough with that fragile male ego of yours. I didn't stick around the next morning, so what? I assume you've done that before, too."

He crossed his arms over his chest and smirked. "No, I haven't."

"Probably because you have a lot of trouble getting women to sleep with you since…"

Since you look fucking perfect.

He smirked again, like he could read her mind.

"Since your personality leaves a lot to be desired," she said at last.

"But my body is perfect?"

"You have an enormous ego."

"I thought you said it was fragile."

She sighed. "What did you come here to tell me?"

"We're finished, if you'd like to take a look."

"That was fast. You better not have half-assed it."

"Don't worry. We didn't."

She got out of the car, but Alex didn't step back as much as he should have, and she nearly knocked into him. But she refused to give him the satisfaction of a curse or a dirty look. She walked away without a backward glance.

Iris inspected the rebar and formwork, and she was happy to see that everything looked good. When she turned to look for Alex, he was right behind her. She hadn't heard him approach, but at least she managed not to scream this time.

Instead, she made an inarticulate sound.

"You're wound up pretty tight," he observed mildly. "Perhaps you haven't had enough sex lately."

"Were you going to offer to help me with that problem?" He started to speak, but she held up a hand to stop him. "Please. Don't bother. I can take care of my own sexual needs, thank you very much."

"Mm. I hope they've *vibrated* the concrete enough. You know if they haven't—"

"Thank you. I am well aware of the problems with concrete that hasn't been properly *vibrated*."

"Does the rebar meet your approval?"

"Yes. Go ahead and pour the concrete."

"When will you be back on site?"

The concrete would have to set for a week after it was poured, and then they would do tests to make sure it was okay before they started on the steel structure.

"Probably not for another two weeks," she said, "but we'll be in touch before then. You'll be corresponding with me instead of Emma from now on."

"I can't wait," he deadpanned.

"I'm sure you're very excited about my return."

"Very excited for you to see how the *steel erection* is going."

"I wish the entire building was made of concrete," she muttered before stomping back to her car. She whipped off her hardhat and safety vest and tossed them in the trunk, then unlaced her steel-toed boots.

God, every time she saw the word "steel" in the next month—which would be quite often, given her profession—she'd think of Alex and his steel muscles.

With any luck, she wouldn't think of his erection, but that was probably too much to ask.

7

IRIS TOOK off her shoes in the front hall of her grandmother's house and put down her bag before entering the kitchen.

"You're home!" Ngin Ngin was stirring something on the stove. "At last. You said you'd be home at six or six-thirty, and it's seven now."

Seven o'clock was the time Ngin Ngin had said she'd have dinner ready every weekday.

"Sorry," Iris said. "I had to get something out today before I left, and I had to spend longer than expected at the hospital."

Ngin Ngin frowned. "Why were you at the hospital?"

"We're doing an addition at East Markham Hospital. I have to stop by every now and then to make sure everything is going well."

"Is that the Charles Fong Cardiology Wing? I heard about this."

Iris nodded. "That's it."

"Charles Fong has three sons. Little older than you. Maybe you will meet one of them. I think the oldest is a billionaire. Maybe you prefer billionaire over man who owns landscaping company?" Ngin Ngin frowned again. "Actually, I think the oldest son has a girlfriend now, but third son got rich from selling tech company."

"Ngin Ngin! Enough with the matchmaking."

"Just saying. It's a possibility."

"I doubt his sons will be there, and I am not up to date on the gossip. I have no idea whether they have girlfriends or not." She paused. "It smells really good in here."

"Pad Thai," Ngin Ngin said. "I learned to make it at the Thai cooking class I took last summer, remember?"

A few minutes later, they were sitting at the kitchen table with their food.

"Wow," Iris said after her first bite. "This is amazing."

"I know. I make good Thai food."

They ate in silence for a few minutes.

"It's nice to have you here for dinner," Ngin Ngin said. "I looked forward to it all day."

Aw. This was why she was living with her grandmother. Comments like those melted her steel heart just a little.

No more thinking of steel, Iris.

"How was your day?" Ngin Ngin asked. "You do good engineering work?"

"I spent most of the day writing a report."

"You have to do much writing as an engineer? I thought engineering was all about numbers."

"I often have to write reports, too."

"How about trip to hospital? How was that?"

"It was…fine."

"You hesitated. I think it's not fine." Ngin Ngin picked up some noodles with her chopsticks.

"Just the site supervisor I have to work with."

"You don't like him?"

"You could say that."

She didn't hate Alex. She just hadn't planned on ever seeing him again, and he'd been rather infuriating today. Their conversations had been completely different from when they were at The Thirsty Lumberjack. She didn't remember there being this much sniping three weeks ago.

Ngin Ngin grinned. "This could be an enemies-to-lovers story. I know all about these things. I see it in movies and read it in books. I started reading Harlequin romance novels, did you know? They're short and easy to read. Well, I assume they're easy for you to read. For me, still a bit of a struggle, but I can do it. And many books have a man and woman who are enemies, then go to bed together."

"Alex and I have already gone to bed together," Iris muttered.

Shit.

She was having dinner with her grandmother, not Crystal or Rebecca, and she didn't need Ngin Ngin knowing about her sex life. She'd spoken quietly, though. With any luck, her grandmother hadn't understood.

"Wait." Ngin Ngin dropped her chopsticks. "You already slept together?"

Well, today just wasn't her lucky day, was it?

"Just once," Iris said. "Before I knew I'd be working with him."

Actually, they'd had sex twice, both times on the same night, but Iris wasn't going to correct herself.

"He's not good in bed?" Ngin Ngin asked. "Is that why you only did it once?"

"This conversation is ending. Right now."

"Aw. I thought it was a great conversation!"

"Not a great conversation to have with my grandmother, no."

Ngin Ngin drew her eyebrows together. "Can't think of the right word. Just a minute. I wrote it down yesterday—I found it in the book I'm reading." She hobbled to the living room, then came back a minute later with a sheet of paper. "*Vicariously.* Yes, that's the word. I live vicariously through you."

"I'm happy to tell you about certain things," Iris said. "Like going out to the bar and going dancing. But some parts of my life are off-limits."

"Where did you meet this man the first time?"

Iris looked down. "At a bar."

"So you can tell me all about it!"

"Nope. Not happening."

"What's his name?"

"Alex."

"Is he a white man? Like Elliot and Connor and Robert Redford?"

"No."

"Black man like Jonathan?"

"No."

"You know who Sidney Poitier is? He made movies many years ago. I think he's handsome. What do you think?"

"Alex is Chinese," Iris had another bite of pad Thai. "What did you do today, other than making me dinner and looking forward to eating with me?"

Ngin Ngin shook her finger. "I know what you're doing. You changed the subject. I will let you, just for tonight. While you were at work, I read the newspaper, plus chapter of Harlequin romance novel. Then I went to see Mrs. Yee and buy bean sprouts for pad Thai. Then I ate lunch and had a nap. Then I watched the weather channel and tried to figure out how to make Netflick work so I can watch more Robert Redford movies, but could not figure it out. You show me after dinner, okay?"

"Okay."

"Maybe afterward, you can also tell me more about Alex?"

"There's no reason for me to do that."

"You know, I won't be around forever. Am very old. One day, I will be dead, and you will say, 'I wish I told Ngin Ngin about hot Chinese man I slept with!'"

"Somehow, I don't think I'll ever say that," Iris said, "and I suspect you won't be dying anytime soon."

"You're right. I will be like Kirk Douglas and live to triple digits!"

～

Alex scowled at his beer. He'd ordered a stout with raspberries because it was the only stout on the menu, but it was too damn fruity. Not like the alcoholic juice Iris had ordered, but still. He didn't like fruit in his beer. He should have gone with the smoked porter instead.

It had been four weeks since he'd met Jamie and Eve at the bar, then brought Iris home with him. He hadn't seen his friends since—and he hadn't spent very long with them last time. He'd suggested they go to The Thirsty Lumberjack again, since it had twenty-four beers on tap, but now that he was here, he regretted it. He kept thinking about Iris, and besides, there wasn't anything great on tap. Too many damn IPAs.

Jamie and Eve came in and sat across from him, their hands linked.

"Hey, man," Jamie said. "I hope you don't plan on deserting us after fifteen minutes again tonight."

"I'm sorry about that. I—"

Jamie waved this off. "No, no. It was fine. Eve and I still had a great night. Did you see that woman again? What was her name?"

"Iris. Just a one-night stand, but apparently she's one of the engineers for the project I'm working on now. She'll be coming to site every week or two."

Jamie slapped the table and laughed. "Oh, man."

Alex had a sip of his subpar beer, then looked toward the bar, half-expecting to see Iris in her midnight-blue dress. If he was honest, the main reason he'd suggested meeting at The Thirsty Lumberjack was because Iris might be here. He desperately wanted to see her again, and at the same time, he desperately *didn't* want to see her. And of course he wasn't counting down the days until her next site visit.

Of course not.

"It was bad," he said. "I accidentally told another guy at work that we'd slept together, and she was pissed. I may have also said some inappropriate things to her."

Eve gave him a look. "Alex!"

"I know." He scrubbed a hand over his face. "It was a mistake. I won't do it again."

It hadn't been like him to say such things, to make lame jokes about vibration and steel erection. There was just something about Iris, something that made him crave getting a reaction out of her. She had an expressive face, and she was easy to annoy, and... It was just so much fun, and he didn't have much fun these days.

Well, that was no excuse. He needed to act professional on site and make sure he didn't make her feel uncomfortable, no matter how many jokes about pipe and drilling and steel erection were just begging to be told.

"So." Alex needed to change the subject. "How have you two been?"

As soon as he asked the question, the waitress appeared, and Jamie and Eve placed their orders before Jamie answered Alex's question.

"We're good," he said. "Looked at a bunch of venues for the wedding."

"There's an old theater on Mount Pleasant that's now an event venue," Eve said. "That's probably what we'll end up doing. Edwards Gardens was my first choice, but they're booked up for the dates we want."

"What about you?" Alex turned to Jamie. "What's your first choice?"

Jamie shrugged. "They're all nice. I'm happy with whatever Eve wants."

"When he said I could do whatever I wanted," Eve said, "I threatened to book a petting zoo."

Jamie looked over at her and smiled.

Alex wasn't jealous of what they had. He'd never been particularly keen on settling down, much to the frustration of his mother, though it wasn't like he had a wild bachelor life.

What he wouldn't give to have his mom bug him about girls again. It had always annoyed him, especially when she'd tried to set him up with the daughters of her friends. Unlike Alex, his mother had been a social person who'd had a lot of friends, and there was never any shortage of women she wanted to fix him up with. He'd always said no, and now he wished he'd said yes once or twice, even though he was certain nothing would have come of it.

Because now his mother was gone and they'd never have an argument again.

"Alex?" Eve said. "Are you okay?"

He'd never get to tell his mother about Jamie and Eve, either —they'd started dating a few weeks after her death. His mother had regularly asked for updates on Jamie.

He's getting married! Can you believe it? He's never dated a woman for more than two months before, and now he's engaged after six months and he loves his fiancée so much that he would even get married at a petting zoo if that was what she wanted.

Alex had taken the fact that he could talk to his mother for granted. He'd never been terribly enthusiastic about giving his mother updates on his few friends and hadn't understood why she kept asking.

His dad, on the other hand, never asked and didn't even know the names of his friends. A few months ago, Alex had been talking to his father on the phone, and after a long pause in the conversation, he'd mentioned Jamie's new girlfriend, not sure what else to talk about. His dad's reaction had been, "Who's

Jamie?" Which wasn't what Alex had been looking for, though he shouldn't have been surprised.

He wasn't adjusting well to his so-called "new normal."

"I'm fine," Alex said.

Eve looked skeptical, but she let it go.

Jamie had a sip of his beer, then leaned forward. "Got a question for you," he said, a little more stiffly than usual. "Will you be one of my groomsmen? It would mean a lot to me."

"That's awful mushy, coming from you," Alex said.

Jamie shrugged. "Will you?"

"Of course." He smiled at his friend.

They chatted for several minutes about wedding food and flowers and favors, and other things Alex had never thought much about before. He tried to provide thoughtful opinions, but his mind wandered.

Hey, Mom. I'm going to be one of Jamie's groomsmen. And you'll never guess what happened to me. I met a woman at a bar called The Thirsty Lumberjack. Stupid name for a bar, don't you think? Her name is Iris, and we...well, we went on a date. Now we have to work together, and I act like an idiot when she's around. We piss each other off. I think you'd like her. You two would come up with great plans to annoy me.

Not that he would have said those exact words to his mother, and of course he never would have mentioned something like a one-night stand.

But dammit. He wished she was here to try to drag information out of him again.

He missed a lot of things that, only a year ago, he never would have imagined missing.

8

IRIS HAD RECEIVED word that the tests on the concrete samples were complete and all was good, so a week after her first visit to East Markham Hospital, the steel construction started.

A few days after that, she was at the office, getting ready to head to site to see how things were going. She was not looking forward to this. She had lots of things to do at the office, and the last thing she needed was to see Alex Kwong again.

"I really don't want to go," she muttered.

Emma looked up from her computer. "Why not?"

"I have lots of drawings I need to go over this afternoon, and..."

Emma got up and walked the short distance between their desks. "Are you having a problem with any of the people on the project?"

Iris hesitated.

"Is it Alex?" Emma asked. "I only met him a couple times, and he was always nice to me, but of course, that doesn't mean..." She looked away.

Iris knew exactly what her co-worker was thinking about.

Earlier that year, Emma had confided in Iris that Dave, one of the other engineers at Lowry, had been harassing her for months. Emma had told him repeatedly to stop, to no effect, and she was thinking of finding a new job. She'd been reluctant to tell their boss, Scott Lowry, but Iris had convinced her to do so before she started sending out resumes. Scott had believed every word Emma had said—the texts and Facebook messages probably helped—and fired Dave. The next day, Scott had called everyone in the office into the meeting room and emphasized that such behavior was not to be tolerated and if there were any problems, he wanted to know, whether it pertained to one of his employees or someone else they had to work with.

At least her employer seemed to have their backs. That wasn't as common in the workplace as it should be. Iris had heard many awful stories of human resources refusing to do anything.

She considered herself fortunate. Even though she had an older white man as her boss, which was fairly common in engineering companies, she didn't feel like she had to work harder to prove herself because she was a woman. Scott had never treated her inappropriately, and he wanted to do everything possible to make sure she didn't face harassment in the workplace. He was hardly what one would call friendly, but he'd always treated her fairly.

"Alex isn't harassing me," Iris said to Emma. "It's just…" She lowered her voice. "We, um, slept together. Before we knew we'd be working together—we met at a bar. It's a little awkward, that's all."

Emma's eyebrows shot up, but she didn't say anything.

"I can handle it," Iris said.

"Are you sure?"

"It's fine. It's only once every week or two. Don't worry, it's not affecting my ability to do my job."

She could have done without some of his comments, though. Like his complaints about her leaving before he woke up. If he did that again, she would tell him to stop, and she suspected he would listen.

But as it turned out, she didn't have to say anything.

She went to East Markham Hospital and met Alex by the trailer. He walked around with her as she looked at the progress to date, and everything he said was related to the project, aside from some small talk about the weather. He did say "steel erection," but with absolutely no innuendo, and it was a perfectly reasonable thing to talk about given the subcontractor was, in fact, erecting steel.

She was almost disappointed.

He walked her back to her car afterward. "I want to talk to you."

Her heart rate kicked up a notch at that.

Alex was handsome—she hadn't changed her opinion there. He'd look better without a hardhat, but that was true of pretty much everyone.

"I apologize for my behavior last time," he said, "and I promise I won't bring up that night again or make any more inappropriate comments. You don't have to worry about that. I also told Carlos not to tell anyone. I'm not sure whether he listened, but he's the rebar guy, and I doubt you'll have to see him again. I will have no problems working with you, and if I do anything to make you uncomfortable, please let me know."

She nodded at him. "Thank you." She appreciated that they could be professional about the whole thing, and she respected him for admitting the error in his ways.

Still, she wouldn't have minded a little teasing, just at the end.

It was another week before Iris returned to site. She was signing in at the trailer when Alex walked over to her, and her skin heated as he approached. He was wearing a blue shirt under his safety vest today, and dammit, she wanted to see him without all the construction gear. The corners of his lips turned up slightly when he saw her, but it barely qualified as a smile.

"Hello, Iris."

"Alex."

They walked around and she made sure everything was as it should be. They were on schedule so far, but there would inevitably be delays at some point. There always were.

"Just one thing that needs to be changed," she said, stopping at the south side of the building under construction. "The mechanical layout has been adjusted, so some adjustments were made to the structure, too…"

She and Alex talked about it for a few minutes. Satisfied, she started back to her car, and Alex hurried to catch up to her.

"You don't have to walk me to my car," she said. "It's broad daylight, and I'm quite capable of walking fifty meters by myself."

"I know I don't *have* to," he said, "but I want to. However, if you don't like it, tell me right now, and I won't do it again."

She stopped and looked at him. They were a few paces from her car. His eyebrows were drawn together slightly; she didn't want him to look quite so serious when he was with her.

"I like it," she said at last.

Something flickered in his eyes. "Good."

She felt a flutter in her stomach at that single word. "It would serve absolutely no purpose for us to talk about why I left so early that morning, but if you want to make comments about steel erection that aren't entirely to do with construction… Well, I would be agreeable. As long as nobody else overhears us, of course."

Although their banter had annoyed her the first time on site, she missed it now. She wanted to have a joking conversation about drilling and vibrations, and this completely serious, non-teasing version of Alex bothered her. It didn't feel natural.

"Hmm." He rocked back on his heels. "Have you...vibrated any concrete lately?"

She rolled her eyes. "That was terrible."

"Have you...thought about me while vibrating your concrete?"

"You wish," she said, opening her car door.

He smiled at her as she sat down behind the wheel, then waved as she backed out.

What was she doing?

It was the following Tuesday, and Iris was coming to site at the end of the day.

It wasn't like Alex had been looking forward to this for days. He hadn't been wondering what she'd be wearing underneath her safety vest, nor had he thought of a whole bunch of lame sexual construction jokes.

It wasn't like that at all, of course.

Well, he'd thought of a few jokes, but they were horrible and he wouldn't use them.

Iris was game for a bit of flirting, though. She'd made that clear to him last time, and he would be happy to oblige, though he was under no illusions it would lead anywhere.

She arrived at four o'clock. The steel subcontractor had just finished for the day, so there weren't too many people on site.

"How was your weekend?" he asked her as she was signing in. "Did you drink any beer that tasted like juice?"

"As a matter of fact, I did," she said. "You know my friend Crystal, the woman who was with me at The Thirsty Lumberjack?"

He nodded. He hadn't been introduced to Crystal, though he'd seen her talking to Iris.

"She's dating Jared, the guy she met at the bar that night. He's really into the craft beer scene, so I went to another craft beer bar with Crystal and Jared and a few of Jared's friends on Saturday night. I got a flight of tasters, and my God, some of them were terrible. I almost spit out the first one on the guy across from me. But the last one was tasty. You would have considered it alcoholic juice. I thought of you as I drank it."

"Did you, now? What, exactly, did you think about?"

She lifted a shoulder and smiled. "Time for me to get to work."

She walked around and studied her drawings to make sure everything was going according to plan. She found a couple minor adjustments that needed to be made but nothing major.

He walked Iris to her car after she was finished.

"Looks like the steel erection is going just fine," she said.

"I'm glad it meets your approval."

"Mm. It does."

He raised his eyebrows. "Did you see any other *steel erections* on the weekend? Meet anyone at the bar?"

"Wouldn't you like to know." She winked at him.

He was pretty sure she was just playing with him. She hadn't actually gone home with any of Jared's lumberjack friends.

Or maybe she had. It was none of his business, and he had no claim on her. Still, he couldn't help clenching his fists in frustration.

Iris looked at his hands pointedly. "It seems like you have a problem discussing steel erection, which is going to cause a bit of a problem as, unfortunately, the addition to the hospital is made of steel. Bet you're now wishing it was masonry. Or concrete."

"Of course," he murmured. "Then I'd get to make jokes about concrete vibration."

"Perhaps we should stop. We both seem to have the sense of humor of a teenage boy."

"I don't know why you bring out this side of me."

"You do the same to me."

He put a hand to his heart. "That's the most romantic thing anyone has ever said to me."

Alex didn't think it was all that funny, but somehow, perhaps due to his deadpanned delivery, it was enough to make Iris bend over and laugh…which made him think of all the things he could do to her when she was bent over.

When she stood up straight again, she took a tiny step closer to him. It was like they were in a tightly-packed subway car, even though they were surrounded by lots of space. He couldn't help but breathe in sharply at her closeness, and he inhaled her scent. Something floral. He wasn't quite sure what, but he remembered it from the night they'd spent together. The next morning, he'd smelled it on her pillow.

But as tempting as it was, he wouldn't kiss her now.

Even if they were both okay with making comments that were somewhat sexual in nature—and even though he'd already slept with her—they were working together.

Besides, although she was flirting with him, she'd left him early in the morning. He doubted she was interested in a repeat experience, even if she'd resisted the charms of Jared's friends, who, in his mind, were all strapping men with big beards and ridiculous man buns.

It wasn't like he wanted more than sex anyway. He'd never had any interest in a serious relationship; the idea of being that close to someone had never appealed to him. His mother had told him that he just hadn't met the right woman yet, and one day, he would meet her, and everything would change. However, since his mother's death, he'd had even *more* trouble imagining that happening. He felt even more detached from the world.

Except when…

He pushed that thought aside.

"Alex?" Iris said. "You okay? You seem a bit spaced out."

"I'm good. Just thinking about…pipes and drilling. Yes, drilling."

"You're a nut. But don't you dare try to work 'nut' into a dirty sentence." She climbed into her car.

"See you next week."

He didn't say anything about how much he was looking forward to it.

9

WHEN ALEX GOT home from the gym on Saturday morning, planning to hop in the shower and then make something for lunch, he heard some strange noises in his apartment. His first thought was a burglar, but he quickly pushed that thought aside. It was likely just his father with another box of food.

Sure enough, he walked into the kitchen to find his father pulling out a bag of snow peas.

Dammit. Why had he given Dad a key to his apartment?

"Ah, there you are." Dad deposited the snow peas in the crisper. "Where were you?"

Alex gestured to his sweaty shirt. "At the gym."

"You sure seem to spend a lot of time at the gym these days."

Yes, he'd had a strong need for physical activity in the past several months, but he didn't mention that now.

Dad pulled out a package of frozen wontons and opened the freezer. "Your freezer is full."

"Because you keep bringing me food I don't need."

Dad somehow managed to shove the wontons into the freezer, then took a package of Rainbow Chips Ahoy! cookies out of a box on the table. "These are your favorite, aren't they?"

What the…

"They were my favorite when I was, like, six. You're almost thirty years behind the times." Alex was thirty-three now.

"Ah. Perhaps I should listen to Madonna on cassette tape."

Was that…a joke?

Alex didn't know how to respond to his father cracking jokes.

"You don't need to keep bringing me food," he said.

"You work out all the time." His father gestured at him. "You must need to eat a lot."

"Most of the things you bring me, which I assume you buy because they're on sale, aren't the sort of things I eat on a regular basis. Like pomelos, for example."

"They're good for you. They have lots of vitamin C, don't they?"

"So does orange juice."

Dad frowned. "Are you saying I should buy you orange juice rather than pomelos?"

"No, I'm saying you don't need to buy me any food. I can do my own grocery shopping."

Some of the things his father gave him would just end up in the garbage. Some he'd give to the foodbank, but he couldn't do that with the perishable stuff.

Dad nodded. "Okay. I understand."

They were silent for a minute, and Alex felt guilty. His father was just trying to be nice, but he really didn't need a dozen packages of wontons in his freezer.

It was all so awkward between them now, but maybe it always had been. He just hadn't noticed because whenever he saw his father, his mother was always there, too. They were rarely alone together, and they hadn't talked much on the phone, either.

"I meant to ask you something," Dad said. "You had a friend… his name starts with J. I can't remember it now. I met him once or twice."

"Jamie," Alex said.

"Yes. Jamie. I meant to ask you how he was doing."

This was a very odd conversation.

"Jamie is fine. Actually, he's engaged, and they're planning to get married next summer."

"Ah," Dad said. "That's good. Very good. Actually, that reminds me of the other thing I mean to ask you. Do you remember the Moks?"

"Um, yes." Alex hadn't seen them in a decade, but they'd been friends of his parents.

Actually, now that he thought of it, they'd been at the funeral. That was a bit of a blur to him, though.

"Do you remember Rose, their youngest daughter? She's five years younger than you."

"Sure. I remember Rose."

"I was wondering…" Dad ran a hand through his hair, then adjusted his glasses. "Well, we were talking, and we were thinking, maybe we could set you up with her. Would you like that?"

Alex looked at his father like he'd grown three heads.

"You're trying your hand at matchmaking," Alex said faintly. "I can't believe it."

"Well, it wasn't my idea. It was Jan's." Jan was Rose's mother. "But I said I'd ask you. Rose is a pharmacist—did you know that? She had a boyfriend for a few years, but Jan says he wasn't a very good guy. They were living together, and one night, he just…left. Wrote a note saying he'd found someone else, and Rose found it in the morning."

"Right. I see."

"So, what do you think?"

"I think," Alex said slowly, still not quite able to wrap his head around this weird conversation, "that I do not need my father interfering in my love life."

Dad nodded and didn't try to change his mind, which was a relief.

"Do you have one?" Dad asked.

"Have what?"

"A love life."

"Sure. I go on dates on occasion." Alex hoped that answer would be the quickest way out of the conversation. Saying he had no love life might cause his father some concern.

He felt like he was in the Wild West, and there were no rules anymore.

At least, the rules that governed how he and his father interacted seemed to have gone out the window. He had no idea how to predict what was coming.

"I was just wondering," Dad said, "if maybe dating had been tough for you since…"

He didn't finish the sentence. He never did. Never mentioned Alex's dead mother, even though she was a looming presence in every conversation. It was like Dad thought he would upset Alex by mentioning her, but Alex didn't see how that would be any worse than the way it was now.

It wasn't like either of them would forget her.

The only time Dad had actually said her name was when they went to the cemetery for the Ching Ming Festival—Tomb Sweeping Day—in April. Otherwise, he just ended his sentences with "since" or "before," and Alex knew what he meant.

"I forgot," Dad said. "I didn't actually tell you anything about Rose Mok other than what happened with her ex-boyfriend. She's a pharmacist—wait, I already told you that. She likes traveling, badminton, and fine dining, and Jan said something about her being interested in cosplay, but Jan also said I shouldn't tell you that." He ran his hand through his hair again. "Anyway. Too late. Do you know what cosplay is? I had to look it up."

Alex shut his eyes for a moment. When he opened them, he said, "Rose sounds very nice, but I'm not interested."

"Why not?"

"Like I said, I don't need you interfering in my love life."

"Has another girl already caught your eye?"

Alex immediately thought of Iris and how they'd frantically ripped off each other's clothes.

"No," he said.

His mother would have detected the lie and pushed him for the truth, but that wasn't what his father did.

"Okay," Dad said. "Are you sure you're not interested in Rose? Is the cosplay thing a little weird? When I was looking it up on Google, I saw some pictures of..."

Alex was tired of telling his father "no," so he let him babble on about cosplay for five minutes while he looked through his cupboards and fridge to see what other food Dad had brought with him, other than wontons and snow peas and cookies.

Iris popped into his head again when he saw the packages of rice crackers. She popped into his mind often these days. He wondered what she was doing this weekend—perhaps drinking more alcoholic juice while wearing a stunning midnight-blue dress?

When Iris woke up on Saturday morning, Ngin Ngin wasn't home. She often went shopping in Chinatown on Saturday mornings and met Mrs. Yee at the bakery. In fact, Ngin Ngin's social life was about as busy as Iris's.

Iris had breakfast, then cut the grass—Jonathan wasn't here to do it today.

Thank God.

She'd lived here for several weeks, and it wasn't going too badly, now that Ngin Ngin had stopped forcing young men to parade around shirtless in her backyard. Iris got delicious home-cooked dinners, and she ate them with her grandmother, rather than with the company of the TV. She felt like she was getting to know a different side of her grandmother, which was nice. Plus,

Ngin Ngin was always in bed by nine-thirty, so Iris had peace and quiet for a couple of hours every night.

After cutting the grass, Iris went up to her room and set up the Kindle she'd bought for her grandmother. Her grandmother complained about the small font in the books she got at the pharmacy, so Iris had bought her an e-reader, which would allow her to use any font size she wanted. Ngin Ngin had eventually learned how to use Netflix on Iris's smart TV, so hopefully she would be able to master the Kindle soon enough, although many things that Iris found intuitive were not intuitive at all for Ngin Ngin, since she hadn't grown up with technology.

Iris bought a few books to get her grandmother started, and when she heard the door open, she headed downstairs with the Kindle.

Her grandmother wasn't alone. She was talking to someone.

"Wait here," Ngin Ngin said. "Will go upstairs to get Iris, then we can have tea."

Oh, no.

Iris hurried down the stairs and found her grandmother, who was putting on her slippers, as well as another elderly Chinese woman and a young Chinese man.

After several weeks without any shirtless young men appearing in the backyard, Iris had been lulled into a false sense of security. She'd thought Ngin Ngin's matchmaking days were over, but clearly she'd been mistaken.

Why else would there be a young man in the front hall?

"Iris!" Ngin Ngin beamed. "Just in time. This is my friend, Mrs. Yee, and this is the grandson I told you about. His name is Roger."

Right. The proctologist.

Roger had a large head and a skinny frame. He wasn't as attractive as Jonathan, and he didn't hold a candle to Alex. She had no interest in watching him cut the grass shirtless. With any luck, he'd be just as unenthusiastic at the prospect of this meeting as she was.

He bowed and kissed her hand. "I'm charmed."

Charmed? What an odd thing to say. He was wearing a tweed jacket in July, which also struck her as odd, as well as oversized glasses. He seemed rather bug-like. Actually, there was something about him that reminded her of a grasshopper, but she couldn't quite explain it.

"Um, hello."

"You look as lovely as a peony."

Iris didn't respond. That was the first time she'd ever been compared to a peony, and although she liked peonies, she found the comparison strange.

She didn't want to be rude, but she really wanted to get out of this situation.

Also, Roger smelled like licorice, and she'd always hated licorice.

"Iris is just shy," Ngin Ngin said. "Don't worry, she talks."

Iris couldn't remember the last time anyone had called her shy. She'd just lost her voice because she was horrified by the situation.

"Iris!" Mrs. Yee said. "Long time, no see. I met you once when you were a small child. You stuck a soybean up your nose. I never forget."

"Aiyah," Ngin Ngin said. "Don't tell stories like that in front of Roger! We want him to like Iris. Also, my grandson tried to stick salted egg yolk up his nose. Much worse. Soybean not so bad."

Roger just smiled as though this was all perfectly normal, and Iris was struck with the horrifying thought that maybe the Yee family was much weirder than her own family.

Not that she'd ever become a member of that family, but still.

"We brought many things from the bakery," Ngin Ngin said. "Go, Iris! Make us tea, and then we will eat, and you and Roger will get to know each other. It will be fun, yes?"

Iris went to the kitchen, where she started the kettle and put some tea leaves in the bottom of a teapot. They would have tea and pastries, and then she'd try to shoo Roger and Mrs. Yee out the door.

"Iris," Ngin Ngin hissed as she approached from behind. "Not that teapot. Use nice one."

Iris sighed and took out the other teapot. "I told you. No matchmaking."

"You're being silly. Cannot tell your grandmother not to matchmake! It's like telling fish not to swim or kitten not to be cute. Or dragon not to be dragon-like."

Soon they were all sitting around the dining room table with small cups of tea. Iris had put the pineapple buns, coconut buns, and egg tarts on a glass platter.

"This is delicious tea, Iris," Roger said. "I must confess, I was led to believe you were completely useless in the kitchen."

"See, this is why Roger is perfect for you," Ngin Ngin said. "He likes cooking."

"I'm not so useless that I can't make *tea*," Iris muttered. "So, Roger, what do you like to cook?"

"Oh, a little of this, a little of that," he said. "My deconstructed dumplings are a thing of beauty."

Deconstructed dumplings? Did that mean the filling was outside the wrapper? And if so, didn't that defeat the entire purpose of dumplings?

"He's very talented," Mrs. Yee said.

"When you get married," Ngin Ngin continued, "Roger can do cooking and Iris, you can do dishes and vacuuming. Like we do now."

Iris choked on her tea. Her grandma was already talking about her getting married to this guy?

"I have no problem with that," Roger said, smiling.

He wasn't disturbed by this conversation about marriage. How odd.

There was a knock at the door.

"I'll get it!" Iris jumped up, happy for the interruption. She wouldn't mind listening to someone try to sell her duct cleaning for ten minutes.

But when she opened the front door, she was faced with something much, much worse.

Her mother, Mrs. Yip, and a man whom she assumed was Mrs. Yip's neurosurgeon son.

Iris rolled her eyes.

"Iris!" Mom hissed. "Don't roll your eyes. It's not attractive, and I've brought a very nice young man who wants to get to know you. This is Phillip Yip."

Phillip gave her a curt nod. He did not look like he wanted to get to know her at all, judging by the scowl on his face. A scowl that was nowhere near as nice as Alex's.

Iris sympathized. She decided she didn't mind Phillip, although she had no intention of going out with him, of course.

"Come in and meet the others," Iris said, gesturing them inside.

"The others?" Mom squeaked.

"Ngin Ngin brought Mrs. Yee's grandson, Roger, over as well. He's a proctologist."

Mrs. Yip made a face. "A neurosurgeon is better than a proctologist."

"I agree," Mom said. "I don't know what Ngin Ngin was thinking. I can't believe it. Why is she inviting men over for you to meet? Everyone knows matchmaking is a *mother's* job."

Laughter floated down the hall from the dining room. Roger had an ugly laugh. Not that Iris cared, because she had no interest in him anyway.

"I quite agree, Mom," she said. "I don't know why my female relatives insist on setting me up with young men. It's a pain, isn't it?" She nodded at Phillip, who grunted his assent, before leading the new arrivals into the dining room.

Mrs. Yee turned to Ngin Ngin. "You told me it was just us! You didn't say my grandson would need to compete, like on *The Bachelorette*."

Ngin Ngin frowned. "What is *The Bachelorette*? And I had no idea anybody else was coming. Not my fault. Why are you here, Carolyn? You're cramping my style."

Iris suppressed a laugh.

Mom leveled Ngin Ngin with a glare. "It's the mother's job to do matchmaking."

"You only think that because grandmother is often dead and not available, but I'm healthy as an ox. Ninety-one years old and still alive!"

"It's nobody's job to do matchmaking on my behalf," Iris said. "I would appreciate if you all stayed out of my personal life. I know in the old days, things were sometimes done a bit differently, but…"

Mom looked affronted. "I am not old. And I met your father through friends."

"See? You didn't need your mother's help. Plus, there's something called the internet now. Perhaps you've heard of it."

"I heard about this thing called Tinder," Ngin Ngin said. "How does it work?"

Iris sighed. "We are not going to talk about dating apps. Now, everyone, I'll make some more tea, and you can enjoy the food, then get out of here as quickly as possible."

She made some tea in the teapot that her grandmother had deemed unworthy of company and brought it to the dining room, then went back to the kitchen to get another three cups.

"So," Mom said, "who do you prefer, Iris? You like Phillip, don't you? He's a neurosurgeon."

"As you've already told me. More than once."

"Roger is a doctor, too," Mrs. Yee said. "He can cook, and he doesn't scowl all the time."

"Stop scowling, Phillip!" Mrs. Yip hissed. "You're much more handsome when you don't scowl!"

"But I don't want Iris to like me." He turned to Iris. "No offense. I'm sure you're perfectly nice, but I already have a girlfriend."

"*What?*" screeched Mom. She turned to Mrs. Yip. "You told me he's available. Why are you wasting my time?"

Mrs. Yip sniffed. "It's a passing phase. He'll be over her soon."

"No," Phillip said. "I already bought a ring. I'm going to ask her to marry me."

"*What?*" Mrs. Yip jumped to her feet. "You can't do that."

"I'm an adult. Of course I can."

"But she… she…"

Phillip turned to Iris. "My girlfriend is white, and my mom would prefer I marry a Chinese girl. Paula is also an activist who cares about a whole bunch of causes that my mother does not approve of. Then there's the atheism thing…"

Ngin Ngin frowned at Mrs. Yip. "My son married a white woman many years ago. I didn't approve, didn't go to wedding. But I was wrong. You should support your son, if he loves this woman."

"You don't understand," Mrs. Yip said, wringing her hands. "Paula is one of those social justice warrior types. And an atheist!"

"Am confused. What is atheist? What is social justice warrior? I assume Phillip is smart enough to pick a good woman, though. He's a neurosurgeon, after all."

Mrs. Yip shook her head. "Being a neurosurgeon doesn't mean he knows how to pick a woman, and you're just saying all this because you want *your* guy to win."

"No, that's not true!" Ngin Ngin said. "I support interracial marriage. Now, leave my house so Iris can continue talking to Roger. Unless you have a girlfriend, too, Roger?"

Roger shook his head.

"Good." Ngin Ngin turned to Mom. "My choice better is than yours! Take that!"

Mom ignored her and looked at Mrs. Yip. "Is it so bad if his girlfriend is an atheist? Better an atheist than someone who claims to be a Christian but has no compassion for others."

Mrs. Yip merely sniffed.

"Why did you come if you already have a girlfriend?" Iris asked Phillip.

Phillip reached for an egg tart. "I thought if I met a bunch of women like my mother wanted and proved that I wasn't interested in anyone else, maybe she'd—grudgingly, of course—come to accept Paula. But it's hopeless. Do you have a boyfriend your family doesn't approve of?"

"No, I'm single, and *that* is what my family doesn't approve of."

"I approve of almost anyone," Ngin Ngin said. "As long as he treats Iris well. Even woman—that would be okay. Already have gay grandson. But Iris is getting old, and she's never had a serious boyfriend. Or girlfriend."

"I'm not old. I'm twenty-seven. You called Robert Redford a spring chicken, and he's more than half a century older than me. Plus I'm happy being single! Why can't you understand that?"

Mom just shook her head like Iris was a pitiful creature. It didn't make sense to Iris. Her parents' marriage was hardly happy and loving. Why was her mother so bent on her joining the institution of marriage?

Phillip and his mother were now arguing about his plan to marry Paula, and Mrs. Yee and Roger were looking smug. Mom broke off a piece of her coconut bun, then picked up the Kindle that Iris had left on the table.

"Is this your e-reader, Iris?" Mom asked.

"Actually, it's a gift for Ngin Ngin. She can adjust the font size. It'll make reading easier for her."

"You bought your grandmother porn?"

"What? There's no porn. It's just…"

Romance novels, since her grandmother had talked about reading Harlequins. One of the covers had a half-naked man on the cover.

Dear God. And Iris had thought this day couldn't get any worse.

"It's just a shirtless man," Iris said feebly.

"Let me see!" Ngin Ngin said.

"Me, too!" Mrs. Yee said.

Mom didn't hand over the Kindle. "This is inappropriate. I'm disappointed in you. You're supposed to be helping your grandmother around the house."

"She is helping," Ngin Ngin said. "Now give me the book." Somehow, she managed to grab it out of Mom's hands. "Yes, this is a very nice cover, isn't it?"

Mrs. Yee nodded her approval.

"But I don't understand how to read on this." Ngin Ngin shook the Kindle up and down. "You can show me later, Iris. I will read all the sex scenes first!"

Mom glared at Iris, then stood up. "Come on." She looked at Mrs. Yip. "Let's go, since this house has turned into a den of filth, and you failed to tell me that your son already has a girlfriend."

Five minutes later, Mom, Mrs. Yip, and Phillip had left. Mrs. Yee and Ngin Ngin had their eyes glued to the picture of the shirtless man on the screen, and Roger was trying to talk to Iris.

"It appears I've won *The Bachelorette*," he said.

"I'm not a trophy to win, and I'm not interested in you."

"You should at least let me tell you about where I'd take you on our first date."

"I'm sure this is going to be fabulous," Iris muttered. "Tell me."

"I would treat you to a romantic home-cooked meal at my condo. For the appetizer, we would have my famous deconstructed dumplings."

"What makes them famous? Who have you cooked them for?"

"Um. Just myself. But they're delicious. You'll see." He then described, in excessive detail, the rest of the meal. "For dessert, we would go to the new café on College Street that was inspired by the poop emoji."

Had she heard that right? "A café inspired by the poop emoji?"

"Correct." He smiled. "I bet you no man has ever taken you there before."

"How, exactly, does this place work? Does everything look like a turd?"

"It does, but it's all very delicious. So, what do you think?" He smiled with the confidence of a man who usually got what he wanted.

Iris still thought he looked like a grasshopper. Plus, the thought of going to a poop-themed dessert café with a proctologist was particularly disturbing.

"No, thank you," she said. "I don't want to go on a date with you."

"But our grandmothers—"

"I said *no*."

"Iris," Ngin Ngin said. "What are you talking about? What is poo-moji?"

She felt like this day would never end.

10

"AND THEN," Iris said, "Roger told me he wanted to take me to a café based on the poop emoji. I looked it up. It really does exist, and it's called 'Poop is Us.'"

Rebecca put her hand on her large belly and laughed. "What did Ngin Ngin think?"

"She didn't know what emojis were, so I showed her. She was very confused by the premise of the restaurant. As am I, to be honest."

"I've heard of this place," Crystal said. "You can get soft-serve chocolate ice cream in a bowl that's the approximate shape of the poop emoji. They add some vanilla frosting for the eyes and mouth, and black gumdrops for the pupils or...something. We should go there after dinner."

They were at an Italian restaurant in Little Italy. Iris had wanted to have sushi, but Rebecca couldn't eat raw fish because she was pregnant, so now they were having thin-crust pizza instead, and Iris was drinking a large glass of wine.

"Are you saying you would have actually gone out with a man who wanted to take you to a poop restaurant on your first date?"

"I'm not saying I would have gone out with Roger," Crystal

said. "He sounds like a tool. But if I'd been drinking with my friends? I might enjoy the novelty of it."

"Remember I can't have alcohol," Rebecca said, "so I can't get drunk enough for 'Poop is Us.' We're going to the weird gelato place instead. Did you know they have Peking duck ice cream?"

"I think that's weirder than the poop place," Crystal said.

"I beg to differ." Iris picked up her next slice of pizza. "How's it going with Jared?"

"Ohhh." Crystal was practically fluttering her eyelashes. "Jared is lovely. And strong. And rugged. And everything a woman could want."

"You've been seeing him for over a month. That's a long time for you."

Like Iris, Crystal was not usually one for relationships.

Crystal shrugged. "I like him. He doesn't talk much—he has the strong, silent thing going on—but when he says something, you really listen, you know? Anyway, I'm not thinking about where it's going. I'll just keep seeing him until it stops being fun."

"Maybe you'll fall in love," Rebecca said.

Crystal shrugged again, which was interesting. She didn't protest that it wasn't a possibility. "What about Alex? Having fun working with him?"

Iris had a sip of wine. "It's okay."

At first, she'd dreaded each meeting, but now, she didn't mind.

Actually, she was rather looking forward to the next time she'd see him—either Wednesday or Thursday, depending on her schedule. Maybe they'd talk about steel erections some more.

"What are you giggling at?" Rebecca asked, leaning forward.

"Giggling? I'm not giggling."

Rebecca and Crystal looked at her doubtfully.

"I think that was a giggle," Crystal said. "Do you ever pull him behind half-finished walls and kiss him senseless?" She made smooching noises.

"That would be inappropriate."

"Well, do you *want* to kiss him senseless?"

Iris looked away. "I still think he's attractive."

"I'm disappointed I wasn't there the night you two met Jared and Alex," Rebecca said. "You should bring them along the next time we go out. We can have a triple date."

"Sure," Crystal said. "Just don't expect Jared to be a great conversationalist."

"I'm not bringing Alex," Iris protested. "There's nothing going on between us now. We're simply working on a project together. Yes, we slept together once, but it's no big deal."

"Mm-hmm. Are your conversations always one hundred percent about work?"

"No. I mean, you talk about non-work things with your co-workers, don't you? Alex and I had a very interesting conversation about the weather once."

Why did she say that? Crystal and Rebecca wouldn't buy it for a second.

Really, there was no reason to talk about Alex. And yet if Iris was honest with herself, maybe she did want to talk about him, even if she'd never ask him to go on a triple date.

She drowned her sorrows in wine once more.

"You flirt with him, don't you?" Crystal said.

"Not when I'm doing my work! But he always walks me to my car afterward."

"He sounds like quite the gentleman," Rebecca said.

Crystal jumped in. "I get the impression he wasn't exactly a gentleman in bed."

Iris felt her cheeks heat.

"Ooh, you're blushing! You never blush when you talk about men. Or sex. Unless your mother or grandmother is in the room. So, are you going to sleep with him again?"

"I shouldn't. We're working together."

"It's not like you have to see him every day, and it's not preventing you from doing your job, right?"

"You're making this sound so sensible, but it's not. I'm not getting more involved with Alex. We're in a good place right now, and I think having sex with him again would ruin that. We had a one-night stand. That's all it was."

"Are you sure about that?" pressed Rebecca, the happily-married woman. "Maybe it could be something more."

Iris shook her head decisively. "Not happening."

Iris went to site again on Wednesday at the end of the day. The project was behind—it seemed like projects were always behind. A shipment hadn't arrived on time, and there had been thunderstorms both Monday and Tuesday afternoon.

"I blame you for the weather," she said as Alex walked her to her car. "The thunder, the lightning, the heavy rain...I bet that was you. You did it to annoy me. I got soaking wet when I walked home from the subway yesterday."

He gave her a crooked smile. "Yes, I'm Thor. I can control thunderstorms." He spread his arms wide.

"You're a nut." Iris couldn't hide her grin.

"Have coffee with me now?"

She must not have heard that right.

"There's an independent coffee shop nearby," he said. "Just give me ten minutes to finish up here, and then I can leave. Unless you have to go back to the office?"

She shook her head and stared at him. Apparently, she hadn't misheard him after all.

"Why?" she asked.

"Why not?"

"Is this a date?"

"It's not a date. I just thought we could have coffee. I don't want to go home to an empty apartment right now. I'd rather talk about steel erection with you."

"We don't have to talk about *work* when you're off the clock." She paused. "Okay. Tell me where this coffee shop is. I'll head there, and you can meet me when you're done." She opened the door to her car.

Why was she doing this? She'd told her friends nothing more would happen between them.

But he'd sounded lonely, behind those light-hearted comments about steel erection, and she didn't want him to be lonely.

Alex opened the door to the coffee shop and immediately located Iris sitting at a table near the back. Her chin was propped up on her hand, and she was looking out the window. It was the first time in ages that he'd seen her without a hardhat and safety vest. She was beautiful.

Mind you, she was still beautiful with the hardhat and safety vest, but it was nice to see her outside of work.

He hadn't planned to ask her to have coffee with him. The words had just popped out of his mouth; he hadn't been able to help himself.

And now, here they were.

He bought a coffee and took the seat across from her.

"So," she said.

"So." He paused. "I confess, it's weird to have a conversation with you that doesn't involve work."

"There was that conversation when we were trying to get each other into bed." She tilted her head. "*Are* you trying to get me into bed? You said it's not a date, but—"

"I'm not trying to get you into bed. Let's try to have a conversation that has nothing to do with sex. Or work."

They were quiet for a minute.

"My grandmother and my mother are both determined to

find me a boyfriend," she said at last. "In fact, both of them brought men over to meet me on Saturday morning."

She proceeded to relate a ridiculous story involving a proctologist, a neurosurgeon, and some very determined mothers and grandmothers. When he started laughing, she glared at him.

"What?" he said. "You can't tell me that you didn't expect me to laugh when you started that story. Wouldn't you have been disappointed if I hadn't laughed?"

"I suppose. But dammit, sometimes my life just seems like one bad joke."

"I kind of want to try deconstructed dumplings."

She made a face. "That defeats the purpose of dumplings."

"It does, but I'm still curious."

"Do you think I should have gone on the date just for the story?"

At the thought of Iris going on a date with someone who wasn't him, Alex was tempted to crush his coffee cup in his fist, but he held himself back. It would make a mess, and besides, he had no claim on her whatsoever.

Yet they were now sitting in a coffee shop, outside of work, as though he wanted her to be something more.

Maybe they could be friends.

He took one look at Iris's lips and decided it could never be that simple with her.

"I don't think you should have gone on the date just for the story. You've got enough of a story as it is." He had a sip of coffee. "My dad tried to set me up with a girl on the weekend, too. She's a pharmacist who likes fine dining, traveling, badminton, and cosplay. I looked up her pictures on Instagram, and she's very talented. I couldn't believe some of the pictures were actually her."

"Are you going to meet her?"

Was that a hint of jealousy in Iris's voice, or was it just wishful thinking on his part?

"No," he said.

"Why not?"

He held her gaze for a moment, then turned his coffee cup in his hands. "I'm not interested in a relationship."

"Neither am I. What about your mom? Does she try to set you up?"

He swallowed. "My mother died last year."

She reached forward and placed her hand on top of his. "Alex, I'm so sorry."

He nodded jerkily in acknowledgement.

She kept her hand where it was, running one of her fingers up and down his.

"But she did before she got sick," he said hoarsely. "No matter how many times I refused, she would keep bugging me about it." He gave Iris a wry smile. "I miss that. My dad took no for an answer so easily, it was almost disappointing. Actually, I think..." He hesitated. "My father and I don't know how to be around each other without my mother there. I never really had a relationship with him that was separate from her, if that makes sense."

Iris nodded. "It's a little like that with my dad, too."

"She called me several times a week, but I rarely talked to him on the phone. She was the one who decided when we'd see each other, what we'd do. She was also the one who'd take the pictures, so now there are so few photos of her."

He hadn't realized the extent of it until now. His mother had been the one his family revolved around, and now they were all cut adrift. Maybe if his brother lived in Toronto, it would be easier, but Stuart and his wife had moved out west a few years ago. Alex hadn't seen Stuart in months, though he was coming to visit soon.

"It's strange," Alex said, "the things I miss now."

He shook his head. He was getting too melancholy.

Fortunately, Iris found the perfect thing to say.

"What would have happened if you'd gotten yourself a fake

girlfriend?" she asked. "You could have pretended you were in a relationship with me. Would that have been enough to stop your mother's matchmaking?"

He managed a chuckle. It was nice to think about his mom like this. "She wouldn't have tried to set me up with anyone if I had a girlfriend, but I think she would have been able to see right through any fake relationship."

"I can't believe Phillip's mom was determined to set him up, even though he already has a girlfriend."

Alex thought for a moment. "If I was serious about a woman, I'm sure my mother would have liked her. She would have done her best to learn to like her, even if she didn't at the beginning. Though my mother liked almost everyone, so I doubt that would have been an issue. She just wanted me to be happy."

"I don't think that's what my mother and grandmother want. I think they just consider me a failure if I don't hit the traditional milestones. Husband, children, and all that. Frankly, my grandfather was an ass, and I doubt my mother and father are happy together. I don't want that kind of life."

And Alex didn't want to feel the pain of loss ever again.

He'd managed, though. In the days afterward, he'd been the only one who hadn't cried. The one who made the funeral arrangements, the burial arrangements. The one who put the obituary in the paper. He had separated himself from that pain as best he could, like he could put his heart in a box and stuff it in the closet.

It hadn't worked entirely, but it had worked well enough.

It still worked well enough.

Sometimes, it was all he had.

He was afraid that if he lost his ability to detach himself, everything would collapse, and there would be nothing left.

Nothing.

"Alex?" Iris said. "Would you prefer to talk about something else?"

Maybe if they were in bed together—not having sex, just her naked body around his—he would be able to say something more, but not here, not like this.

He gave her a sharp nod.

"Okay," she said. "What are your hobbies? I assume they're not traveling, fine dining, badminton, and cosplay?"

He managed a smile. "I like food, of course. Just not if it's deconstructed. Or in the shape of a poop emoji. I like traveling, but I haven't been anywhere in a little while." Not since his mom had gotten sick. "I work out a lot."

She rolled her eyes. "That's obvious. The first thing I noticed about you was your biceps."

"Not my gorgeous silky locks?" He touched his hair, which he kept quite short.

"You could be in a shampoo commercial."

"You think so?"

"To be honest, I think you're hot enough that you could sell anything."

"Mm. What should I try to sell you today?"

She smiled at him. She had the loveliest smile he'd ever seen, no doubt about it. He wanted to see it again and again, but he also liked making her roll her eyes or glare at him.

"I'm sorry," she said. "I can't stay much longer. My grandmother is expecting me home for dinner."

Alex walked Iris to her car. When they reached it, he stepped toward her and lifted his hand, and she gave him a barely-perceptible nod. He touched her cheek, stroking the pad of his thumb across her skin.

"Thank you for today," he said before gathering her in his arms and pressing his mouth to hers. She tasted of warm milk and coffee. It was comforting to kiss her, to be with her, even though they had talked about things that weren't so comfortable.

She moaned against his lips and swept her tongue into his mouth. She bit his bottom lip.

"You're going to be the death of me," he said when she pulled back.

Apparently, that made her want to kiss him again.

Well, he wasn't complaining.

This time, she wrapped her arms around him and took control of the kiss, of the give and take, of the pressure, ending with a light brush of her lips over his.

"I'll see you next week," she said as she climbed into her car.

"When will you come to site?"

"Probably Wednesday."

And then she was gone, and he could only think of next Wednesday.

11

"You're quiet today," Ngin Ngin said at dinner. "Cat got your tongue? This is a new expression I learned."

Iris shrugged, then picked up a snow pea with her chopsticks.

"What happened at work?"

"Nothing. Work was fine."

"I have many, many decades of people telling me they're fine when they're not. You tell me the truth!"

Iris chuckled.

She really *was* fine. She was just a bit out of sorts after that kiss. After that conversation with Alex at the coffee shop. She wasn't used to being out of sorts because of a man.

Something he'd said the night they met jumped into her mind.

I want to take you to my bed and use you to forget...

Now she knew what he'd wanted to forget.

"Ngin Ngin," Iris said slowly, an idea forming in her mind. "Can I have a friend over next Friday for dinner?" She felt like a child, asking questions like this.

Ngin Ngin put down her chopsticks. "A friend? Is this friend a man?"

"Yes."

"What's his name?"

"Alex."

She hoped her grandmother had forgotten who Alex was. Unfortunately, she wasn't that lucky.

"Alex," Ngin Ngin said. "This rings a bell... Yes! I remember. He is the site supervisor at your job, and you slept together!"

"Um."

"Is he your boyfriend now? Is this why you want me to meet him?"

"He's not my boyfriend," Iris said. "Women are allowed to have male friends, you know."

She would not mention today's kiss. She would not.

God, she couldn't believe she was bringing a man to meet Ngin Ngin. It wouldn't matter how much she protested. Her grandmother would treat Alex as though he was her boyfriend.

But it would make Ngin Ngin happy, since she desperately wanted Iris to get a man. With any luck, it would also make Alex happy, since he seemed lonely and he missed having interfering female relatives. Iris was sure Ngin Ngin was nothing like his mom, but she thought he might enjoy it.

This wasn't entirely selfless, though. If Ngin Ngin met Alex, perhaps she would stop her matchmaking efforts. Iris didn't want to be surprised by any more proctologists and their grandmothers coming over for tea, or by a man cutting grass shirtless in the backyard. (Unless it was Alex. It would be no hardship to see Alex cutting the grass without a shirt.)

She just hoped Ngin Ngin wasn't already planning the wedding.

"What should I cook for him?" Ngin Ngin asked. "What does he like to eat?"

"I don't know. Anything you like. I'm sure he's not too picky."

"This is not a helpful answer."

"Whatever you want to make. It doesn't need to be fancy. I feel bad asking you to cook for another person, but—"

"Better me cook than you." Ngin Ngin grinned. "You would scare him off with your terrible cooking. Plus, you might blow up the kitchen."

"Thanks, Ngin Ngin."

"It's okay, I don't mind making dinner. Not every day I get to meet Iris's boyfriend."

"He's not my boyfriend!"

~

"You want me to come over for dinner?" Alex asked after walking Iris to her car the following Wednesday. "Come over for dinner and meet your grandmother?"

He hadn't thought they had this sort of relationship.

She nodded. "That's right."

"Am I your fake boyfriend now?"

"Nope. In fact, I've told my grandmother about five hundred times in the past week that you are *not* my boyfriend, which of course makes her even more convinced that you are." She shrugged. "I just hope it means Roger won't be coming over again, because I do not need a repeat of that."

He didn't understand why this was happening, but he wasn't going to say no to Iris.

"I'll be there."

~

After work on Friday, Alex drove to the address Iris had given him. It was an old, narrow house near Chinatown. He parked on the street, got the box of chocolate from the backseat, and headed to the door.

It was nice to have something to do on a Friday night rather than being brutal to his body at the gym, then going home and making a quick dinner and collapsing in front of the television.

Still, he couldn't help but be nervous.

He knocked on the door and immediately heard yelling inside, which made him smile. A minute later, Iris opened the door, and his skin prickled at the sight of her. She was wearing jean shorts and a T-shirt, which made him feel slightly over-dressed—he'd changed after work and put on a dress shirt.

"Hello," she said. "Come in."

An elderly Chinese woman with short white hair appeared beside her. "You are Alex?" After he nodded, she turned to Iris. "I think you made a good choice. Your boyfriend is very handsome."

"For the last time, he's not my boyfriend."

"Is this true?" Iris's grandmother asked him. "You're not her boyfriend?"

"I am not."

"Aiyah. Silly kids. It reminds me of oldest granddaughter, Natalie. She kept insisting Connor was not her boyfriend, and now they're married." She took the chocolate from his hands. "This for me?"

"Yes."

"I like this kind. Very tasty." She looked him up and down. "Yes, you are nice. I forgive you for not being a medical doctor like Connor. You have an engineering degree, like Iris?"

"No," he said. "I have a diploma in construction engineering technology."

She frowned. "You have no degree? Your parents allowed this?"

Well, they hadn't exactly been thrilled.

"Stop it," Iris said, laying a hand on her grandmother's shoulder. "Alex is fine just the way he is."

"Ah, I understand." Iris's grandmother nodded sagely. "You have other talents. I read naughty books that Iris bought for me on my Kindle. I know all about these."

"Ngin Ngin!" Iris said.

Her grandmother laughed and turned around, shuffling into the house. "Alex, you can call me Ngin Ngin, too. I'm old now. That's what everybody calls me. Soon, maybe I will even forget I have another name!"

Twenty minutes later, the three of them were seated around the dining room table with plates of tortellini and green salad, as well as chopsticks and jasmine tea.

"My friend is Italian. She taught me to make pasta," Ngin Ngin said, lifting a piece of tortellini with her chopsticks.

"It's very good." It wasn't what Alex had been expecting, but it was certainly tasty.

"You have any grandparents left?" Ngin Ngin asked.

He shook his head.

"Well, now you have me!" She grinned. "You born in Canada?"

He nodded. "My mother got pregnant with me soon after my parents came here from Hong Kong."

"You speak Cantonese?"

"Yes, but not well."

"Probably better than Iris's Toisanese."

Iris nodded. "This is true."

"She understands a bit," Ngin Ngin continued. "But speaking? Not good at all. And she can't read. All she knows are the characters on mah jong tiles. I have many more questions to ask you, Alex. Are you ready?"

He hid a smile. "Okay."

"How old are you?"

"Thirty-three."

"Thirty-three and not married?" She shook her head. "Must get working on that. When will you propose to Iris?"

"Ngin Ngin!" Iris exclaimed. "I already explained. We are not a couple."

"Then why did you bring him to meet your grandmother?" Ngin Ngin shot back. "You never brought a man to meet me before."

"I haven't lived with you for very long. It's different now that we live together."

Suddenly, Alex understood why Iris had invited him over. Because she thought he needed this, thought he needed the teasing, the bickering…the feeling of being part of a family, interfering relatives and all.

He squeezed her knee in gratitude.

"I saw that!" Ngin Ngin said. "You're touching. You must be a couple. When you get married, where will you live? You can live here. I don't mind. Alex can do yard work without a shirt. I will enjoy it."

Iris shook her head. "I can't believe you."

"I'm teasing! Why do you not like my jokes? But am serious about the first part—you can both live here with me. At nighttime, I take off my hearing aid, so if you make noise in bedroom, I won't hear."

Alex dropped the piece of tortellini he'd held in his chopsticks. He had no idea how to respond. His mother wouldn't have said something quite like *that*.

He glanced at Iris, who was turning as red as the tomatoes in the salad.

He had to admit, he enjoyed seeing someone else rile her up.

"Okay, okay," Ngin Ngin said. "I'll stop now. I'm worried Iris will never bring you here again, Alex, so I must behave." She paused. "What about your parents? Are they retired?"

"My father works for a bank. My mother is dead."

His parents used to talk about what they'd do when they were old and retired. Now, Alex wasn't sure his father wanted to retire at all.

Ngin Ngin frowned. "That is sad. Sorry I brought it up. When did she die?"

"You don't have to keep asking questions," Iris said.

"It's okay," he said. "She died eight months ago."

They were quiet for a minute, focusing on their food. Iris poured everyone more tea.

"You have other relatives in Canada?" Ngin Ngin asked.

"Just my father and brother. Some of my relatives are in California, some in Hong Kong."

"You must marry Iris right away. Then you will have big family in Canada!"

He chuckled. "What was Iris like when she was little?"

"Iris was only grandchild who lived in Toronto as a kid," Ngin Ngin said. "I saw her lots but could not communicate well because my English wasn't good then. We drew lots of pictures together, and I sewed her clothes. Now I sew clothes for great-grandchild. He will be born very soon."

"My cousin is pregnant," Iris said, turning to Alex. "She's due in a few weeks."

"She's big like watermelon! I think maybe she's having twins."

"No. The doctors would be able to tell if she was having twins. They would see it on the ultrasound."

"I will tell you a story about Iris," Ngin Ngin said. "When she was five, she stuck a soybean up her nose."

"Oh my God," Iris said. "Please stop. I thought you didn't want to tell stories like that in front of men because you didn't want to scare them off."

"But you tell me over and over, 'Ngin Ngin, Alex is not my boyfriend.'" Ngin Ngin raised the pitch of her voice when repeating Iris's words, even though Iris's voice wasn't that high. "Now I finally listen to you."

Iris just hung her head. "You see what I have to put up with?" She turned to Alex.

"I will tell you another story," Ngin Ngin said, "since apparently you and Iris are not together. If you were her boyfriend, it might be discouraging, but if you are a *friend*, it's different. You see, Iris is very bad in the kitchen. She cannot even make toast."

"I can make toast!"

"Fine, fine, you can make toast and boil water, but that's about it. Anyway, first kitchen disaster was when Iris was six years old. I tried to be cool Canadian grandmother and make chocolate-chip cookies with her. I got the recipe from a friend, and we were making cookies, all was good, except Iris sprayed batter on the wall when she turned on the electric mixer at the wrong time. But that wasn't the biggest problem. No, biggest problem was when Iris realized her rainbow bracelet was missing. She started crying, we looked everywhere for it. Finally, I took the cookies out of the oven and saw it baked into one of the cookies. Beads were starting to melt. How we didn't notice, I'm not sure. She was so upset because it was her favorite bracelet. I bought her a new one, but she said it wasn't the same."

Alex started laughing, and Iris glared at him. He wanted to kiss that glare off her face, but he wouldn't do that in front of her grandmother, of course.

"Anyway," Ngin Ngin continued, "this was the beginning of Iris's problems in the kitchen. One time, she exploded my rice cooker!"

"Okay, okay," Iris said, laying a hand on top of her grand-mother's. "That's enough. How about I clear the dishes and serve dessert?"

"What is your favorite dessert?" Ngin Ngin asked Alex, then continued without waiting for an answer. "I made tiramisu. I hope you like it."

"You made tiramisu?" Iris said. "Wow, that's impressive."

"Wait until you taste it to give compliments. But I tried a little already, and it's very good. Every time Alex comes over, I will make something special."

"Oh, you don't need to do that," he said.

"Ah, are you saying you will come another time?" Ngin Ngin beamed. "That makes me happy."

By eight-thirty, Alex had eaten three portions of tiramisu at Ngin Ngin's insistence. It was, indeed, delicious. Ngin Ngin had gone upstairs to read and said she would take out her hearing aid so he and Iris could do "fun things," at which point Iris had made a totally horrified expression. Now they were sitting on a couch that looked like it was from the seventies, with its brown and orange color scheme.

"Was that okay?" Iris asked him, concern on her face. "You hardly got a chance to say anything."

"It was good," he assured her. "I'd missed that. When it's just me and my father, there's too much silence." He pressed a kiss to her cheek. It had been difficult to avoid touching her and kissing her all through dinner.

"It takes so much energy to deal with her, as well as my mother, but…" She looked down. "I would miss it. It's true."

He thought of what he didn't have anymore, and he pulled Iris onto his lap so she was straddling him. He held her as tightly as he could.

I wish you could have met my mother, he almost said, but he held the words back.

Instead, he kissed her again and lost himself in the kiss. He slid his hands underneath her shirt and circled his thumb over her nipple. Her hands slipped under his shirt as well, brushing over his abs, and he hardened beneath her.

He'd seen her several times in the past month, but aside from the kiss last week, he hadn't touched her until today. Now she was here, in his lap.

With a groan, he pulled himself back. "We should stop before things go too far."

"Too far?" She gave him a saucy smile. "What's wrong with that?"

He could hear his heart beating in his chest. "You want to go to bed with me again?"

"I always did," she said, her voice catching a little. "And

tonight, I won't stop myself from having what I want. But not here. We'll go to your apartment."

They stumbled into Alex's apartment and immediately started kissing. It was like last time: he pressed Iris against the door and kissed her hard, pinning her hands to the side as he devoured her.

It was like last time, and yet it wasn't.

She'd been a stranger in a bar, and he'd brought her home because they liked the look of each other and wanted to fuck. He'd asked about the ring on her pinky finger, what kind of engineer she was, and she hadn't answered.

Now, he'd seen her at work.

He'd seen her with her grandmother.

He'd been alone with her, when they weren't getting ready to have sex.

Alex rocked his hips against her. Slowly, deliberately, his erection pressing into her stomach. Her breath caught.

"Iris," he said. Just her name, nothing more.

He continued to rock his hips as he kissed her, sliding his lips down from her mouth to her throat, to the top of the simple T-shirt she wore. She trembled against him and shut her eyes, tilting her head up to expose more of her neck as he kissed his way back up to her lips.

He needed her so badly, in a different way than he'd needed her before.

Now, it mattered that it was *her*. It wasn't simply about satisfying their basic needs.

He let go of her wrists and reached for the bottom of her shirt, pulling it off in a hurry, and then undoing her bra and throwing it to the ground. Her nipples were tight, pebbled, and he dipped his head and sucked one of them into his mouth, which made her gasp and clutch his back. He shifted to the other nipple.

"Alex," she groaned, her fingers clawing at him.

When he released her nipple, she unbuttoned his shirt and her hands were on his bare skin. It was a relief to feel her right against him, and yet it made him more desperate at the same time.

He watched her face as he unzipped her shorts and slid his hand inside her panties, his middle finger stroking from her clit down to her entrance and back again. She arched against him.

"Alex," she said again.

"You have a very small vocabulary when I'm touching you."

"I…"

He smirked as he pushed a finger inside her before she could finish that sentence.

"You're an ass," she said.

He immediately withdrew his finger and held up his hands. "If you think I'm such an asshole, I can stop touching you."

"Damn you," she muttered.

He removed her underwear and shorts before touching her again. She was wet for him, and he easily thrust two fingers in and out of her as she struggled with his belt and the fastening on his jeans.

And then she wrapped her hand around his cock.

"Oh, God," he said.

She moved her hand up and down. She used a gentle touch, such a gentle touch, and yet it was enough to ignite a fire within him. He fucked her more roughly with his fingers, and she squeezed his dick as she shattered. It took everything within him not to finish then and there. But he wanted to finish inside her.

He held her as she came back down. "You ready?"

She nodded, her head jerking unsteadily, and he pulled a condom out of his pocket and rolled it on. They were both breathing rapidly now.

"Do it," she whispered.

He picked her up and brought her down on his cock.

Oh, sweet heaven.

She wrapped her legs around him. He didn't move for the longest time; he just held her against him. He was inside her; she was all around him, and nothing mattered except the fact that she was with him—he felt terribly, terribly lucky.

As he started to pump inside her, he held her gaze, and it was almost too much, but he couldn't look away. For so long, he'd been living in a shadow, and now she was *here*, and everything was vivid and bright and topsy-turvy.

He clung to her and walked toward the bedroom, where he set her down on the bed, still inside her. She was on her back, her legs still wrapped around his hips, and he thrust into her again and again. She made the most precious moans. He buried his face between her breasts and lavished attention on them. She was so perfect beneath him, this little spitfire of a woman who took whatever she wanted, and he had the power to make her whimper and thrash as he fucked her.

He slowed his pace as he started thrusting more deeply, wringing out everything he could from the union of their bodies. She pulled his head down toward hers and kissed him frantically.

"So good," he murmured, then pressed his lips back to hers.

He touched her clit as he sped up again, and when she came beneath him, he shoved into her a few more times and found his own release.

Afterward, he went to the washroom and took off the rest of his clothes before joining her in bed, his body curled around her. She was shivering, despite the warmth of the summer night, and he pulled up the blankets so they were cocooned together.

"What are we doing?" she asked.

"Lying in bed."

"Smart ass. You know what I mean."

"We're sleeping together." Which was also a non-answer, just stating the obvious, but he didn't quite have an answer for what she was asking.

What was happening between them…it frightened him because it wasn't something he was used to, because he'd spent the past year forcing his heart into a box. Yet it was okay that he didn't have the answers, because she was in his bed, and if she was with him, everything would turn out okay.

They were quiet for several minutes. He trailed his hands over her breasts, over her stomach, and lost himself in the feel of her body, without the desperation he'd had before.

However, when she started rubbing herself back against him, he got hard again almost instantly. He turned her onto her back and rolled on top of her. She giggled as he nuzzled her hair.

"You want me to fuck you again?" he asked.

"Yes, please."

"You've developed manners. This is new."

She swatted his back.

"I'll do it," he said. "Under one condition."

"What is it?" She sounded ready to do just about anything.

"You have to stay the night." He nuzzled his way down her neck. "I don't want to wake up in the morning and find myself alone in bed." In fact, he didn't think he could bear it if that happened.

"I'll stay the night. I promise."

That was enough to make him feel like he'd won the lottery.

12

WHEN IRIS WOKE up the next morning, she was warm and cozy. Not because Alex was wrapped around her—no, he was on the far side of the bed. They were not touching at all.

The reason she was warm and cozy was because she'd stolen all the blankets during the night. She blamed it on the fact that she wasn't used to sharing a bed. She didn't do relationships, and though she had one-night stands on occasion, she didn't always spend the night.

And now she had all the blankets and Alex had none…and he was naked. He lay on his back, one arm thrown over his head, his legs spread slightly, which gave her quite the view.

Mm.

At four o'clock in the morning, she'd woken up to go to the washroom, and when she'd come back to bed, he'd been awake, too. They'd made out in the darkness of the room, and he'd kissed his way down her body and given her another orgasm and made her promise, once more, that she would be there in the light of the morning.

Now it was seven-thirty, and she was here. She wouldn't sneak out like last time, and she'd let him sleep for a little longer.

After admiring his naked form for another minute, she slipped out of bed and went to the front door, where she found her clothes from yesterday in a pile. She put them on, then checked her phone.

Her mother had sent her several text messages. There were three pictures, two of shirts and one of the most hideous pair of shorts Iris had ever seen. Who wore orange shorts?

Apparently, Mom had purchased all of these clothes for her. In all likelihood, they had been on sale and couldn't be returned. Iris sighed. Her mother liked to do this. No matter how often Iris protested and said that she was twenty-seven years old and didn't need her mother to buy her clothes, her mother didn't listen. On occasion, Mom found something that wasn't bad, but in general, the stuff she bought wasn't at all to Iris's taste. Like the orange shorts.

Iris texted her mother. A moment later, her phone buzzed.

Call me, the message said.

She glanced toward the bedroom, where Alex was sleeping. If she went to the far end of the living room and spoke quietly, hopefully that wouldn't be enough to rouse him.

"Iris!" Mom nearly shouted when she answered the phone.

Iris held her phone away from her ear. "Could you stop screaming? It's really not necessary."

"Why are you whispering?"

Because I'm at a guy's apartment, and he's still sleeping.

"No reason," Iris said, not in the mood for scandalizing her mother this morning. She raised the volume of her voice just a touch. "Why did you want me to call?"

"I want to know what you think of the clothes."

"The shorts are super ugly."

"They're *retro*."

"Whatever." Iris curled up on the couch and hoped this conversation wouldn't be too long. "The shirts are okay."

"You know, being enthusiastic wouldn't kill you."

"I'm enthusiastic. Just not when talking about retro clothes before eight o'clock in the morning. I haven't had my coffee yet."

"I have something else to tell you, too. Your father and I were talking, and we thought maybe one of the reasons you weren't interested in Phillip was that you don't like Asian men."

Iris didn't know where to even start with this. And her father and mother talking…that was more like her mother talking and her father occasionally nodding his head.

"The problem with Phillip," she began, "was that he already had a girlfriend. Or perhaps she's his fiancée by now."

"That *was* unfortunate, but did you like him otherwise? He's cute, no?"

"He's okay."

"I know you're used to Western standards of attractiveness, but—"

"Oh my God. *Mom.*"

"The men you think are more than okay—are they all white? Like the guy I met at your apartment, the one with all the tattoos…"

Iris was getting a headache. "Stop it."

"Perhaps you should open your mind a bit."

A part of her wanted to snap a photo of Alex lying in bed—above the shoulders, of course—and send it to her mother to shut her up.

Nothing would shut her mother up, though.

"My mind is sufficiently open," Iris said. "For your information, I have no problem with Asian men, Chinese or otherwise—didn't we already have this discussion after Natalie's wedding? My problem is with my mother involving herself in my love life."

"Did you know there's a game show in China where parents pick partners for their adult children? It's quite a hit."

Iris shuddered. "How awful."

"Anyway, I really think you should try expanding your mind."

Listening wasn't her mother's strong point.

"You know what would expand my mind?" Iris muttered. "Drugs."

"Iris!"

"I'm kidding."

"I sure hope so," Mom said, and Iris could picture her look of disapproval. "What was I saying... Oh, yes. I've found a very nice white man for you. His name is Ivan, and he's an engineer like you. Computer engineer, I think. Anyway, I have to go. See you later!"

"I hope you're not planning to bring him over today."

But her mother had already hung up.

Iris put down the phone with a sigh. Her mother really should have had more kids so she would have more people's lives to interfere in. Alas, her parents had struggled to conceive.

Her thoughts returned to the naked man lying in bed. The man whose apartment she was in. The man who probably missed bickering with his mother.

She felt a strange pressure in her chest.

She did love her mother, and her mother loved her, even if their relationship was complicated and often revolved around arguing.

Iris started a pot of coffee and looked in the fridge to see what Alex had to eat. When she saw he had eggs and butter, she decided to make him scrambled eggs. Wouldn't he enjoy waking up to a home-cooked meal?

Then she heard her grandmother's voice in her head. *Iris is very bad in the kitchen.*

True, something like eggs Benedict was out of the question, but Iris could manage scrambled eggs. She'd made them many times for herself before. What could go wrong? It was difficult to screw up scrambled eggs.

She broke two eggs into a bowl. Unfortunately, the third egg didn't break the first time she knocked it against the counter, and on her second attempt, she knocked it too hard and the egg white and yolk came out of the shell and dropped onto the floor.

She'd ruined one egg, but that was okay. She'd clean it up and continue.

A couple minutes later, there were four eggs in the bowl, and she'd beaten them with a little milk. She turned on the frying pan and added some butter. Once the pan was hot, she dumped in the eggs. She poured herself a cup of coffee, then figured she ought to wake Alex up, seeing as his breakfast was cooking and it was after eight o'clock.

She went into the bedroom and lay down next to him, draping her arm across his body and pressing a kiss to his cheek.

"Hey," she said.

"Hey, yourself." He opened his eyes and pulled her into his arms. "It's nice to see you first thing in the morning."

His words made her warm inside.

Jesus, this man was turning her into a marshmallow. Making her feel warm inside, inspiring her to cook him breakfast…

She even experienced a momentary longing to have a real relationship with him.

"If you're wondering why you don't have any blankets," she said, not wanting to dwell on those thoughts, "it's because I stole them in the night. When I got up, I didn't put them over you because, well, you look so nice when you're naked."

"Mm. Is that so?"

His words were rough with sleep. God, he had such a sexy voice.

He rolled on top of her and rocked his hips against her, his erection pressing between her thighs. Yes, that was good. They would fuck, and she would forget her budding feelings for him. Having sex was a very sensible plan.

He slipped his fingers between her legs and spent a long time giving her even more pleasure than he had in the middle of the night. She was just coming down from her second orgasm when he said, "I smell something burning."

Just then, the smoke detector went off.

"Shit!" She jumped out of bed. Her legs were unsteady, but somehow she managed to make it to the kitchen and pull the pan of burnt scrambled eggs off the element.

Alex chuckled as he joined her by the stove and wrapped his arms around her. "So it's true. You really are a disaster in the kitchen."

"It's your fault."

"My fault?"

"You were so…so…*sexy* that I felt compelled to cook for you."

"You know, if someone hadn't stolen the blanket in the middle of the night, you might not have noticed how sexy I am. And it's not like I forced you to cook. Or to wake me up while you had something on the stove."

"I was planning to head right back to the kitchen after I woke you up, but you distracted me. You *touched* me. And *kissed* me. *Everywhere*."

"That sounds truly awful. I'll have to remember never to touch you and kiss you again." He doubled over in laughter. "I can't believe you screwed up scrambled eggs. Scrambled eggs!"

"If you keep laughing, I'm not going to let you have any coffee, and I did *not* screw up when I made the coffee. My coffee is delicious!"

She tried to sound offended by his comments, but she was secretly pleased she'd made him laugh so hard, even though it had involved her burning breakfast. Soon, she was laughing along with him. If anyone had been there to see them, it would be quite a sight: two naked people, laughing their heads off in the kitchen.

"Unfortunately," she said once she'd calmed down, "there are only two more eggs in the fridge. There would have been three, but one of them slid onto the floor when I cracked it open."

"We'll go out for breakfast." He looked in the direction of the bedroom, then turned back and winked at her. "After we finish what we started." He swept her up into his arms. "I promise to kiss and touch you *everywhere*."

∼

Alex did indeed fulfill his promise of kissing and touching her everywhere.

Happily sated, Iris relaxed against the pillows as he headed to the washroom, but when he came back, she jumped out of bed.

"All right, let's go out," she said.

He chuckled as he wrapped his arms around her waist and pulled her back into bed. "Why the rush? Do you have anywhere else you need to be today?"

"No…"

"So stay here with me, just for a little while."

"Um, okay."

He held her from behind and pulled the sheet up to her waist.

"Just like this?" she asked.

"Yes, just like this."

"I don't get it."

He sighed. "You're always moving. You always have something to do. Try doing nothing for a little while."

"I'm not much of a cuddler."

He sat up and scrubbed a hand over his face. "Fine. We can go out for breakfast now."

Dammit, she missed his body heat. "No, not yet."

She pulled him back down, and as he wrapped his arms around her, she thought that maybe she could get used to this cuddling business. When she was with a guy, all of the ways they touched were usually sexual. But although she was naked now, this was different.

Alex was right. She was always moving, always staying busy.

She didn't even have the patience to wait for scrambled eggs to cook.

She considered trying to start a conversation, but in the end, she just luxuriated in the press of his chest against her back, his strong arms, the soft sheets, the sunlight streaming through the thin curtains. She was simply in this moment with him, enjoying the sensations.

"Okay now?" he murmured.

"Yes," she said. "More than okay."

When Iris got home after having a late breakfast with Alex, Rebecca was sitting on the couch next to Ngin Ngin.

"I've been sewing for the baby," Ngin Ngin said, holding up a tiny green shirt.

"You don't need to." Rebecca laid a hand on her grandmother's arm.

"Of course I don't need to, but I want to! What do I have to do all day, other than make sure Iris isn't burning down the kitchen?"

"I'm standing right here," Iris said, not saying anything about the kitchen she'd nearly burned down that morning.

Ngin Ngin looked up and smiled. "How was your night? You had good sex?"

"Ngin Ngin!"

Rebecca muffled her laughter with her hand.

"I'm not stupid," Ngin Ngin said. "I know what you were doing."

"That doesn't mean you need to say anything about it."

"I know, but it's fun to tease you. I'm not judging, don't worry. If I was sixty years younger, I'd do the same thing. Alex is very handsome and polite. I approve."

"I can't believe you brought Alex to meet Ngin Ngin," Rebecca said.

"Neither can I," Iris muttered, but after a moment of thought, she decided she didn't regret it. She'd done it because it seemed like he missed having an interfering female presence in his life. Not that anyone could replace his mother, of course, but she'd thought her grandmother would make him smile. And she had.

"You use…" Ngin Ngin paused, like she was searching for a word. "Flogger? Handcuff? Sex toy? I read about these on Kindle. Is this what all young people are doing these days? BDSM?"

"What sort of books did you buy her?" Rebecca asked.

"Nothing with *floggers*."

"I bought books myself," Ngin Ngin said. "Dee showed me how. This one I'm reading now, it has a black cover with red roses. Very artistic. No roses in the book, though. It is…interesting. I like Kindle. I make big font. Good for my old eyes, and I can buy books without walking to the store."

Dear God. The e-reader had been a mistake. Iris imagined her grandmother bringing up BDSM at a family gathering, and she would have to explain how Ngin Ngin had gotten such knowledge.

"Can we talk about something else?" Iris asked as she sat down on the couch beside Ngin Ngin. "Anything else? Please?"

"Fine, fine. You are a prude. You only talk about this stuff with Alex." Ngin Ngin tapped Rebecca's laptop, which was sitting on the table. "You were going to show me Facebook, yes? That's why you brought this?"

Rebecca nodded. "Simon put up a bunch of pictures of Livvy. I thought you'd want to see them." She opened Facebook and clicked on one of Simon's photo albums. They went through the pictures, starting with a couple of Livvy at Natalie's wedding.

"She looks so sweet in that dress," Ngin Ngin said. "And she called me pretty! I know she called everyone pretty, but still."

Next, there were a couple pictures by the water in Stanley Park, including one of the whole family: Seth, Simon, and Livvy. There was also a picture of Livvy at some sort of music class for toddlers, and another of her sitting in a swing, wearing a serious expression.

"You help me learn to use the computer?" Ngin Ngin turned to Iris. "I want to use Facebook so I can look at pictures myself."

"You don't need to," Iris said. "I'll make a point of showing you the pictures whenever Simon posts them, okay?"

"I should still learn. I know you think I'm too old, but I didn't learn English until I was a senior citizen, and now I speak pretty good, no?"

"If I teach you to use the internet, I'm afraid you'll start looking at porn."

"What are you talking about? What is this porn thing?"

"Um," Rebecca said.

"Um," Iris said.

Ngin Ngin laughed. "That was a joke. I know what porn is. I promise not to look at it, just pictures of family. You know what else I want to do? I want to put old pictures into computer. I have albums upstairs. You can do this, yes?"

"I don't have a scanner," Iris said, "but we can get one and do it." It was a good idea.

"Okay. I want to use computer just for Facebook and old photos. I promise, I will do nothing else."

"You know," Rebecca said, "maybe there's a class at the community center you could take. Sometimes they have classes to teach older people how to use the computer. We can look into that for you, okay?"

Ngin Ngin nodded, and they returned to looking at Simon's pictures. There was a photo of Livvy "reading" a book upside down, and another of Seth holding a dinosaur hand puppet up to her face, which made her grin. In the next photo, the dinosaur puppet was pretending to eat Livvy's ear.

Ngin Ngin put a hand to her eyes and sniffed.

"Are you crying?" Iris asked. "What's wrong?" She handed a tissue to her grandmother.

"It's so sad," Ngin Ngin said. "I won't get to see her grow up."

"I know they live on the other side of the country," Rebecca said gently, "but they'll come to visit. They'll be here at Thanksgiving. Maybe Christmas."

"Not what I mean. By the time she's an adult like you, I will be dead. I won't get to see pictures of her graduation or wedding. I only know her as a little girl. She's cute now, but I want to see what she is like when she's older. But by the time she finishes high school, I will be a hundred and eight. Nobody lives that long." She put her hand on Rebecca's pregnant belly. "Your baby, too."

"Maybe you'll live to be a hundred and twenty," Rebecca said, placing her hand over Ngin Ngin's. "Maybe you'll be in the Guinness Book of World Records. You're in good health."

Nobody said anything for a minute. Iris couldn't help but imagine life without her grandmother, and she was sure Rebecca was doing the same.

"I love you," Rebecca said, a tear sliding down her cheek.

"Aiyah," Ngin Ngin said. "Now I make everyone sentimental. I should not think about such things. Rebecca, you cry easily when pregnant? I was like that, too. Both times, I cried over ads on television, even though I didn't understand any of the words!"

That afternoon, Iris located the box of old photo albums in the storage room upstairs and brought them down to the living room. Ngin Ngin was at the bakery with Mrs. Yee, so there was no one to give her the story behind each of the photos.

Iris started with the two albums from her father's childhood. She'd seen them before, but not in many years. The colors were dull and faded, and some of the photographs were torn. It was strange to see her relatives frozen in time like this, the moments preserved decades later—her father as a child, her grandmother as a young woman.

Actually, Iris looked a little like Ngin Ngin had when she was young. There was something about the shape of her face, the way she held herself.

Would Iris look like Ngin Ngin in sixty-four years? Would she even live to be eighty or ninety?

There was a picture of Ngin Ngin and Yeh Yeh at Christmas, a Christmas tree in the background. Another of them at a wedding reception in a Chinese banquet hall. In both pictures, her grandmother was smiling, even though her marriage had hardly been happy. Yeh Yeh's death nearly twenty years ago seemed to have opened up a world of independence and freedom for Ngin Ngin, which she'd embraced. She'd learned things she'd never had a chance to learn when she was young; she'd made so many friends.

Iris would not marry and then wait until she was an old lady to have true freedom. Of course, if she got married—and to her dismay, Alex immediately popped into her head—it didn't have to be like her grandmother's marriage. It probably wouldn't be near as stifling.

Still, it would feel like she was giving up a part of herself, and she refused to let anyone have that power over her. She didn't want a marriage. She didn't want a relationship.

When she'd walked home from the diner after breakfast, she'd had a bit of a spring in her step, and now that unsettled her. She'd invited Alex over to meet her grandmother last night, and she'd slept over at his apartment, eaten breakfast with him, and snuggled up to him.

He was starting to feel like a boyfriend, and for a moment, she'd even liked that idea.

Iris forced herself to take a deep breath. It was okay. She was still in control of her life. They'd spent one rather intimate night together, that was all. She'd cool things off a little. The thought of never seeing him again outside of work was unbearable, but a short break would do them good. Then they could continue to

really was spectacular sex.

ıg at the pictures and tried to push Alex

n't quite succeed.

13

THERE WERE three of them sitting around the table.

Three, not four.

Alex was at a Chinese seafood restaurant in Scarborough with his father and his brother, who was in town for work. Even though Alex was keenly aware that his mother wasn't there, it was nowhere near as awkward as it would be if it was just him and his father.

"The Chinese food here is better than in Calgary," Stuart said as he reached for the scallops with vegetables. "The other day, one of my colleagues told me he liked Asian food. 'What kind?' I asked him, and he seemed totally confused by the question, as though Asia was all the same to him, one big continent with a few billion exotic people." He smoothly moved the conversation to a new topic. "What's new with you, Alex? What project do they have you working on now?"

"An addition to East Markham Hospital," he said before stuffing a shrimp in his mouth. "Been there for a few months now."

"Going okay?"

"Sure. It's fine."

He'd been to East Markham Hospital many, many times in the months before his mom's death. At first, he'd grimaced when he'd learned he was being put on this project, but he'd pushed those feelings aside. It was work. He could manage—and manage he did.

He didn't mention his mother now, nor did he mention Iris. It was Thursday, and he hadn't seen her in almost a week. He wondered when she'd be coming back to site—probably early next week. They'd sent each other a few text messages since she'd left his place on Saturday morning, but not many. He wanted to ask her to come over again, but he felt awkward about it and feared she'd say no. She seemed to have her own set of rules for her life, and he wasn't entirely sure what they were. Yet she'd stayed all night and even tried to make him breakfast the next morning.

He couldn't help but smile at the thought of her screwing up scrambled eggs.

"What's up?" Stuart asked. "You don't just smile for no reason. You got a girl?"

"Sort of," Alex said, before he could think better of it.

His father had probably noticed him randomly smiling, too, but Dad wouldn't ask about such things. Stuart was more like their mother in this respect. In most ways, actually.

"Oh? This is the first I've heard of it." Dad perked up. "And I just saw you on Sunday."

Yes, Dad had stopped by again on Sunday with another box of food. He hadn't brought any frozen wontons or pomelos this time, but apparently apple pies had been on sale, and he'd gotten two for Alex.

"Like I said, I *sort of* have a girlfriend. It's not very serious. That's why I didn't tell you. But somebody"—Alex slapped his brother on the shoulder—"is nosy."

Except, in a way, it did seem serious with Iris, even if she'd only slept over once.

"What's her name?" Stuart asked.

"Iris."

"What does she do?"

"She's an engineer."

"Did you meet her at work?" Dad asked.

"Um, it's complicated. We first met at a bar. And that's all I'm telling you."

Dad seemed to accept this.

Stuart, however, grabbed Alex's phone off the table and found Iris's contact information and picture. "She's pretty. Shall I send her a message and say I'm excited to meet her?"

Alex wrestled the phone out of his brother's hands and stuffed it in his pocket.

"Fine." Stuart held up his hands in surrender before picking up his chopsticks again. "No text messaging, but next time I'm in town, you should invite her to dinner with us."

Alex was about to say he didn't know if Iris would still be in his life at that point. He had no idea how to define their relationship.

But he couldn't get those words out of his mouth because the thought of not having Iris around caused him too much pain.

"How's Ericka?" Dad asked Stuart.

"Oh. About that." Stuart put down his chopsticks again.

Shit. Was something wrong with his sister-in-law? Alex dropped his shrimp and stared at his brother. He couldn't bear it if something else was wrong.

Stuart had a stupid grin on his face, though. "She's pregnant."

Silence.

"Well, come on," Stuart said, gesturing toward himself. "Aren't you going to congratulate me?"

Mom would have spoken in the silence. That was the problem. She was always the first to react, usually with ear-splitting volume. Like when Stuart had announced he was getting married.

They'd had their first Christmas without her. Chinese New Year. Her birthday—she would have been sixty-two. They'd gotten through those milestones, but this type of big news was different.

Alex glanced at the empty chair at the four-person table before turning back to Stuart. "Congratulations. How far along?"

"Twelve weeks. We're hoping to move back to Toronto before the baby comes. I'm not here just for the conference—I also have an interview tomorrow."

His brother was thirty-one, but Alex was having trouble wrapping his mind around the fact that Stuart was going to have a kid.

He was glad they planned to move back to Toronto. Ericka's family was in the Toronto area, too, and it would be good for them to have family around when there was a baby.

Alex would be an uncle.

And his father…

"You'll be a grandfather," Stuart said, smiling at Dad.

The rest of the dinner went reasonably well, but when Alex got home, he didn't feel like himself. He sat at the kitchen table with a cup of tea and a scowl.

This wasn't right. It wasn't right at all.

His mother was gone, and yet the world kept on going, and that shouldn't be possible. She'd never get to hold her grandchildren. She'd never get to spoil them rotten and sneak them extra sweets, and God, she would have been such a wonderful grandmother, and this just wasn't fair. She used to talk about Stuart and Alex having kids one day, in a joking way—it wasn't like she'd pressured them—and now that time had come and she wasn't here.

He rested his elbows on his knees and put his head in his hands, but his hands were shaking.

"Dammit."

He wanted to go to the gym. He wanted to beat his body down physically, and maybe that would give him some respite, but it was nine o'clock at night. He had to be up early tomorrow, and he didn't feel like driving anywhere.

There was also a nearby coffee shop that he liked. It was rarely busy—much to his surprise, since it was a nice place—and sitting on the back patio was soothing, somehow. Unfortunately, it closed at six o'clock.

Instead, he ran up and down the residential streets in the Annex, finding the smallest amount of solace in the activity. The pounding of his feet on the pavement, his heavy breathing. Forty minutes later, he returned home and had a shower, and then he was back to sitting at his kitchen table, feeling like he couldn't stand to be in own his skin, not when the world was the way it was.

He wasn't used to feeling like this.

In the months since his mom had died, he'd always felt like he had some semblance of control, despite the grief. But there was just something about Stuart's news. Happy news, but it had been a punch to the gut, and he couldn't seem to separate himself from it the way he normally could.

He picked up his phone to text Iris, then dropped it back on the table.

Like he'd told Stuart, she was only *sort of* his girlfriend. Asking her to come over now and stay the night, when he was in a foul mood—that didn't feel like something he could ask of her.

He didn't want to talk to Jamie or another friend.

He wanted Iris.

Alex knew he'd feel better with her company. She could distract him better than anyone else. Even when she couldn't completely take his mind off things, somehow she made everything okay. He could *feel* things with her, and yet it was safe at the same time.

It felt like too much of an imposition to ask her to come over tonight, but he could ask her to come over tomorrow after work. Tomorrow was Friday, and if she slept over, maybe she could burn his breakfast again. Or maybe he could simply hold her as the morning light filtered through the curtains.

He texted her, then he stared at his phone for ten minutes, unable to do anything but wait for her response. When she said she was free tomorrow, he let out a sigh of relief.

Tomorrow, he would see her.

The thought calmed him enough that he was able to get some sleep.

As soon as Iris came through his door on Friday evening, they were upon each other, kissing each other, undressing each other, hurrying to the bedroom. Alex needed to feel every inch of her, to lose himself in the physicality of it all.

After he'd found his release inside her, they lay curled up in bed together, his arm around her. They stayed there for a long time without talking, and then he made her wonton soup with bok choy and chicken stock, chopped green onions on top.

His mother had made the chicken stock. She would make a big batch every few months and freeze it in glass jars in the downstairs freezer at their house. It was weird to think of it as Dad's house now, not Mom and Dad's house, and it was only two months ago that Alex had changed the contact in his phone from "Mom and Dad" to "Dad" and deleted her cell number.

There was still chicken stock from the previous summer in the freezer. She'd made it just after she'd been diagnosed with cancer, and Dad had brought over a few jars in his last box of food, her handwriting marking the date on each lid.

Had his father been using the chicken stock? Or was it too painful for him?

Somehow, jars of frozen chicken stock had taken on unbearable significance in their lives. Yet another thing they never talked about.

"This is delicious," Iris said. They were sitting at his kitchen table, eating out of blue-and-white porcelain bowls with matching Chinese soup spoons.

"The wontons are store-bought," he said. "And the stock...my mother made it."

She leveled a gaze at him. "I thought your mother was dead."

"She is, but this was in the freezer. She made it a year ago."

He tried to feel his mother's love in each bite he took, but although the soup was tasty, it was nothing more than simple food.

Iris put down her spoon. "I feel like I should say something deep and meaningful now, but I'm better at snarky comments." She patted his thigh under the table.

"That's okay. You don't have to say anything."

Iris was not the sort of person who made people pour out their hearts and spill their deepest secrets. At least, he doubted other people saw her that way, but there was still something about her that made him comfortable in a way he wasn't with anyone else.

"My brother's wife is pregnant," he said. "He told us at dinner last night, and all I could think was that my mother would never get to meet her grandchild. It was happy, but it wasn't, not really. I felt like shit when I got home, and nothing I did helped at all." *Except when you said you'd come over today. That helped a little.* "Which isn't like me. I can usually push things aside and go on as usual, more or less. In the days following her death, I was so damn *functional*. Now, I don't understand how I did it."

"You did it because you had to, and it felt better than falling to pieces. But you don't have to be strong all the time. You can let yourself feel the way you feel now. You don't have to force it away." Iris shook her head. "Don't listen to me. I don't know what I'm saying."

"No, it makes sense." He reached across the table and covered her hand with his.

I can only let myself feel this way when I'm with you.

14

IRIS WOKE up in Alex's bed again. Unlike last weekend, he hadn't asked her to stay the night; there was simply an understanding between them that she would.

This time, when she woke up at seven-thirty, she didn't attempt to make him breakfast. She looked at things at her phone —thank God there were no more pictures of ugly clothes from her mom—until he woke up, hard, and made love to her. They ate cereal for breakfast, returned to bed, and later, they went for a walk.

"I have something I want to show you," he said, taking her hand.

As they headed to their mysterious destination, she kept glancing at their joined hands. It was so odd to be out in the sunshine, holding a man's hand.

But she didn't let go.

He led her to a coffee shop on Dupont called A Cup of Stars, which she thought was a silly, nonsensical name, though she didn't tell him that. Rather than stopping at the counter, he led her to the backyard patio.

"Perfect," he murmured, and walked to a wooden swing that

was partially obscured by some potted bushes. "Sit here."

She sat.

"I'll get you some coffee," he said. "You take it black, right?"

She nodded. "Why did you want to take me here, rather than Starbucks?"

He sat beside her on the swing and turned her to the right, where there was a white trellis with plentiful pink roses, and then her gaze was drawn by what was above the fence. On the brick wall of the next building was an enormous mural of a little girl standing on a hill, looking up at the night sky.

"Now look to the left," he said, wrapping his arm around her.

On the building to the left, there was another mural, this one a close-up of sunflowers, as well as more roses—real, not painted. There was a light breeze, and it ruffled her hair and brought the scent of the flowers to her nose. Jazz music drifted out of the back door of the café.

She didn't know what to say.

"I stumbled on this place last year," he said. "I never had anyone to bring here, but I thought it was…"

Romantic.

She knew exactly how he was going to finish that sentence.

The unspoken word lingered in the silence between them.

"I come here occasionally by myself," he said. "To take a break from the city. I find it peaceful, but if you want to go somewhere else—"

"No, no." She laid a hand on his thigh. "We can stay."

He was right: it was a lovely little refuge from the fast-paced world.

It unsettled her, though, that he would bring her to this place. It wasn't the sort of thing men ever did for her. If they'd tried, she wouldn't have let them.

Alex went inside, and he came back a few minutes later with coffee and crumbly currant scones that tasted like heaven. She rocked the bench swing gently back and forth, using just the tips of her toes, and she felt almost giddy.

"Would you like me to get you another scone?" he asked after she'd wolfed hers down.

"Yes, please."

When he returned with the scone, he broke off a piece and fed it to her. She closed her eyes as his fingers touched her lips. She took the piece of scone into her mouth and chewed slowly.

Currant scones really were the best thing in the world.

"I like it here," she said as she opened her eyes. *I like it here with you.*

He smiled at her like nothing made him happier than making her happy.

She was still unsettled, but she pushed those feeling away.

"Someday," he said, "I'd like to have a house with a little backyard, though that seems like an impossible dream in a city with such expensive real estate. I'd make it like this, maybe. Without the murals on the buildings next door, of course, but a few pieces of patio furniture, a little garden and climbing roses—I've always thought I would like gardening. A place to relax, an escape from the world, in my own backyard."

"That sounds nice," she murmured, allowing herself to imagine she was part of his future, to wish for things she'd never wished for before.

He wrapped his arm around her, and they simply sat like that for a while, sipping their coffee. A little bird landed on her empty scone plate and pecked at the crumbs, and she laughed.

It was perfect, somehow.

All Alex had done was take her to a neighborhood coffee shop, but it felt like a very special gift.

"What kind of flowers do you like?" he asked.

"I like roses." Really, what woman didn't? "Peonies. Tulips…"

Was he asking because he wanted to get her a bouquet of flowers? Or because he was imagining what flowers he would plant in his backyard garden and wondering what would please her?

She couldn't remember a man ever giving her flowers. Since she didn't do relationships, men didn't buy her red roses for Valentine's, or take her out for a nice dinner on her birthday, or do something sweet for her, just because.

Alex pressed a kiss to her temple. "You're so beautiful."

Various thoughts still niggled at the back of her mind, but she pushed them aside once more and just focused on the man sitting next to her, holding her.

He was so damn handsome, and he really did have the greatest arms. She'd always been a sucker for nice arms.

She closed her eyes, leaned her head on his shoulder, and sighed in contentment. Without him, she couldn't fully appreciate a quiet moment like this.

But this…this was nice.

She looked at the mural of the night sky and stopped herself from wishing upon a star.

By the time Alex asked Iris to have dinner with him, they'd been together almost twenty-four hours, and the strange thing was that she wasn't itching to get away from him. They'd had a leisurely day together, and she'd enjoyed it very much.

However…

"We can have a quick dinner," she said, "but I have plans with Crystal later in the evening. I'm supposed to meet her at a bar on Queen Street."

"Come over afterward?" he asked, raising his eyebrows.

Damn, he was devastatingly sexy and she nearly said yes.

"No," she managed to say, "but I'll see you on Tuesday or Wednesday when I'm on site."

Last night, he'd shown her a different side of himself. A more vulnerable side, and her heart, which sometimes felt like it was made of steel, had ached for him. Yet at the same time, she'd felt that as long as they were beside each other, as long as she could take his hand in hers, it would all be okay.

Then this afternoon, they'd spent an hour at A Cup of Stars, and she'd felt so impossibly close to him in that romantic setting, sitting on the wooden swing bench surrounded by roses.

Now, the spell she'd been under when they were on the back-yard patio was broken, and she wondered why she'd had so many mushy thoughts. What the hell was wrong with her?

Last weekend, she'd decided it would be good to get some distance from Alex, and look what had happened instead. But she hadn't been able to help herself, not with him. She'd resolved that it would be nothing but sex, and yet it continued to feel like something more. It was good she already had plans with her friend tonight, or she might be tempted to spend the entire weekend with him.

"Vietnamese food?" she said, then suggested a nearby restaurant that was pretty casual and not at all romantic.

"Fuck," Iris said as she slid into the seat across from Crystal.

"Is that what you and Alex have been doing lately?"

"Oh, yes. There has been lots of fucking. I also attempted to cook for him, which ended as well as you would expect."

"What happened?"

"I burned scrambled eggs. I know, I know, scrambled eggs are practically the easiest thing to cook, but... Dammit, I need a drink."

They were tucked into a booth at a cozy bar on Queen Street. A good place to have a long conversation, but not a good place if your goal was to pick up a hot man and take him home.

The waitress came around, and Iris ordered a vodka and lime.

She wasn't feeling particularly creative tonight. Crystal, to her surprise, ordered some kind of beer she'd never heard of.

"You're ordering *beer*?" Iris said.

Crystal shrugged. "Jared introduced me to a few things that are pretty good."

"You have so much to tell me."

"Not yet. Don't change the topic. We're talking about Alex."

"Alex." Iris blew out a breath. "At first, we were just seeing each other at work. After our first awkward meeting on site, he was polite and kept things professional, which I should have wanted, but I encouraged him to flirt with me. I couldn't help it. There was lots of talk about steel erection."

"Of course there was," Crystal murmured.

"One afternoon, he invited me to have coffee with him. He told me some rather personal things, and I invited him over to meet my grandmother last week. Since then, we've been sleeping together, but it's not like the first time. It's more than just sex, even though I don't want it to be."

"Would that really be so bad?"

Iris's eyes widened. "That's not the reaction I expected from you. We've had a ton of conversations about how we don't want to be tied down to anyone. What's Jared done to you?"

Crystal smiled to herself. "Oh, nothing. Except for sleeping over nearly every night and giving me an unlimited supply of back rubs and orgasms."

"And introducing you to beer you actually like."

"And that." Crystal paused. "It's been nice. Drama-free, unlike the relationships I had in university, but not boring and… I have no words to describe it. I never thought it could be like this for me, but I think I might actually be in love with him." She looked stunned. "My God, did I just say that?"

"You did."

Iris couldn't help feeling disturbed. She and Crystal agreed on what they wanted in life. They wanted to be independent single woman, free to go out and have fun and sleep with whomever they wanted. They would have their careers and their friends, and sometimes a hot male body to warm their beds. Many men would consider that an ideal life—well, substituting "female body" for "male" in most cases. Why couldn't they do the same?

But now Crystal had Jared, and Iris had Alex. Kind of. Sort of.

"I love him," Crystal said, "and that doesn't freak me out. Huh."

"Well, I don't love Alex," Iris said. "I do like him quite a bit, though. Maybe it's sort of like a friends-with-benefits situation in which we're also working together?"

Ha. No. She couldn't say that after this afternoon, after he'd taken her to A Cup of Stars.

She hadn't been to East Markham Hospital in more than a week. Not since they'd gone out for coffee together for the first time, not since the two nights she'd spent in his apartment.

So much had happened since the last time she'd seen him in a hardhat.

"Fuck, fuck, fuck," she muttered.

"That doesn't sound good," Crystal said, sipping her beer.

"I just realized it's a conflict of interest. It is, isn't it? I'm sleeping with the site supervisor. At first, I thought the fact that we'd had a one-night stand was no big deal, but now, we have a *relationship* of sorts." Iris shuddered at the word. "I don't believe it affects my ability to do my job. I believe I can be objective, but if this comes out, it'll look bad. Really bad."

It was her responsibility to make sure the building was constructed according to the plans. If people knew she was sleeping with Alex, they might wonder if she'd been lenient on any issues that came up with the general contractor because of their personal relationship. And if there were any safety issues with the finished structure, the engineering company's ass would be on the line.

She'd sworn she'd keep her personal and professional lives separate. Never entertained the idea of sleeping with anyone she knew through work.

But then Alex had happened.

"You're right," Crystal said. "That's tough."

They were women—minority women—in a field dominated by men. They faced extra scrutiny. Iris would be judged harshly for this.

Her face heated. She rarely felt shame about her sex life. She'd slept with many men, had lots of casual sex, and she was okay with that.

This was different.

She had feelings for Alex, as uncomfortable as it was to admit. Although she was pretty sure she could be objective, she wasn't a hundred percent sure.

She scrubbed her hands down her face. "I have to tell my boss. Maybe everything would be just fine on the project, but I'd feel guilty about hiding this."

Scott would take her off the project. She didn't think he would fire her, but he would never look at her the same way again, and she hated to lose his respect. He'd always treated her well. He'd always been fair.

Crystal took her hand and nodded sympathetically. "Okay. Let's figure out exactly what you should say."

Iris shook her head. "I'll figure that out tomorrow. Right now, I just want to get drunk and hear about Jared."

But as the conversation drifted to other topics, her thoughts remained on Alex.

Fuck. Relationships—even if they were vaguely defined, even if they weren't super serious and official—always led to problems.

She regretted having more than a meaningless one-night stand.

It just wasn't worth it.

～

"What's wrong?" Ngin Ngin asked Iris at lunch the next day.

"Nothing," Iris said, moving the food around on her plate.

She didn't want to talk about Alex. Didn't want to talk about the conversation she needed to have with her boss on Monday.

"Did you have a nice time with your friend last night? I hope you're not doing any drugs."

Iris laughed weakly. "Don't worry. All we had was alcohol."

There was a knock at the door.

"I'll get it." Iris jumped up and ran to the door.

It was her mother.

God, this was just what she needed right now.

"Iris!" Mom walked in. "I brought the clothes I got for you."

"Uh, thank you."

"Is Ngin Ngin here, or has she left for Sunday afternoon mah jong?"

"She's here. We're eating lunch."

Mom walked into the kitchen, Iris trailing behind her.

"Carolyn." Ngin Ngin nodded. "Nice surprise. Not enough food for you, but you can have tea. Is Lewis here?"

Mom shook her head. "I just came to bring Iris a few things and tell her about the date she has on Thursday."

Iris nearly choked on her tea. "You set me up on a date? Well, I suppose I should be thankful you didn't bring him over for a surprise visit today."

"That didn't work out so well last time," Mom said stiffly.

"Why can't you get it through your head? I don't want to be set up with anyone!"

"I told you about Ivan already, didn't I?" Mom continued, acting like she hadn't heard Iris. "Your date is at Lemongrass. Seven o'clock. Don't be late. I'll show you a picture so you can recognize him. He's cute, I think."

Iris vibrated with rage. "I'm not going on this date, and

Lemongrass is a crappy restaurant anyway. Restaurants that serve Chinese, Thai, Vietnamese, Japanese, and Korean food all together are always suspicious. They're for white people who don't know any better."

"Well, Ivan *is* white. The restaurant was his mother's idea, but I can change it if you have a better suggestion."

"Like I said, I'm not going."

"It's just a first date. It doesn't mean you have to marry him. I didn't interfere in your dating life for the longest time, but now you're twenty-seven and—"

"And, what? I don't owe it to you to get married. I'm happy with my life the way it is."

"You certainly don't sound happy right now."

"Because you're trying to get me to do something I don't want to do!" Iris was tired of repeating herself.

"Aiyah," Ngin Ngin said. "Iris, why don't you tell your mother the truth? You don't want a date with Ivan because you already have a boyfriend."

"I do not have a boyfriend!"

Mom looked at Iris, then Ngin Ngin.

"She brought him over for dinner," Ngin Ngin said. "Nice Chinese man named Alex. Not a neurosurgeon or proctologist, but I think he's good. Very handsome."

Iris put her head in her hands. She could not deal with her mother and grandmother at the same time. Frankly, she was surprised Ngin Ngin hadn't told her mom about Alex sooner. Like the very next morning.

"Iris had a man over for dinner," Mom said slowly. "A man she chose herself, and you say he's *nice*?"

"Yes, he's polite. I told him stories about when Iris was little."

Mom looked like she still couldn't wrap her mind around this. She was probably thinking of the heavily-tattooed man she'd seen at Iris's old apartment at ten o'clock in the morning, a man whom Mom would certainly not describe as polite, though he'd actually been quite considerate.

"Iris tells me repeatedly he's not her boyfriend," Ngin Ngin said, "but she's just being silly. Two nights, she didn't come home until the next day. I know she was with him. And why would she bring him to meet me unless she likes him very much?"

Dear God. This was too much. Iris massaged her temples.

Mom turned toward her. "Is this all true?"

"Yes," Iris said glumly. "Except for the part about him being my boyfriend. Just because it was more than a one-night stand doesn't mean he's my boyfriend."

"But it started with a one-night stand," Ngin Ngin said. "Iris told me this. Then they discovered they're working together. Like plot of Harlequin romance!"

Well, Ngin Ngin's memory was certainly intact, despite her age.

Mom's eyes widened. "I can't believe you brought him to meet your grandmother before your parents."

"Oh, God," Iris said. "Are you jealous of Ngin Ngin? Get over it, Mom."

Mom sniffed. "I'm your mother, and I hadn't even heard about this man until five minutes ago. Why don't you tell me anything?"

"Because he's not my boyfriend."

"Then why did you bring him to meet Ngin Ngin?"

"Because his mother's dead, and I thought he would enjoy meeting someone who was motherly and fussed over him. It's just him, his dad, and his brother now."

"And you chose your grandmother rather than your own mother."

"Less pressure, and I live with Ngin Ngin. But it's no big deal. Because, like I said, *he's not my boyfriend!*"

"It's so complicated these days," Ngin Ngin said. "One-night stand, friend with benefit...all these terms. Anyway, Carolyn, I think Iris cares for this man very much, even if she's confused on terms. You should cancel the date with Ivan."

"Alex and I are over," Iris said, despite the pain the words caused her. "It was just a fling, and now it's over."

"So I *shouldn't* cancel the date with Ivan?" Mom asked.

"Yes, you should! You should stop this silly matchmaking of yours, but not because I'm with Alex."

"Why are you so against having a boyfriend?"

Iris felt like tearing out her hair.

Ngin Ngin frowned. "I don't approve. Why are you and Alex over? He's a nice man for you. He looks at you, how you say it? *Adoringly*. And you brought him to meet me. No matter what you say, I think it's partly because you care for him."

"Stop gloating," Mom snapped. "I heard it the first time. She brought him to meet you and not me."

"What? I'm not gloating. Aren't you impressed I know this word? I learned it from the book I'm reading. It's about—"

"That's enough," Iris said, scared that Ngin Ngin was going to say something about flogging and BDSM. "I refuse to go on a date with Ivan, and there's nothing you can say to convince me otherwise. And Alex is *not* my boyfriend. I don't know why nobody can get that through their heads when I keep saying it over and over."

"I know what the problem is," Ngin Ngin said. "You had lovers' quarrel!"

"You can think whatever you like. I don't care."

"You really are pissy today," Mom observed.

Iris didn't feel like proving her mother's point, so she said nothing and started shoving her food—nearly cold by now—into her mouth.

"Fine," Mom said. "I will leave. Iris, let me know when you've discovered those 'hideous' shorts actually look good on you. Since you're so insistent, I will cancel your Thursday-night date with Ivan, though I really think you should reconsider."

"No, she shouldn't reconsider!" Ngin Ngin said. "She should solve lovers' quarrel and have make-up sex with Alex."

Mom glared at Iris. "I think those books you put on Ngin Ngin's Kindle are a bad influence."

"What you talking about?" Ngin Ngin demanded. "I'm an adult. I can decide what books I read. Iris, I'm leaving soon. Will be gone until five o'clock, so you can have Alex over. If you want him to stay for dinner, that's okay. I'll make good food for him."

"Alex is not coming over," Iris said, gritting her teeth. "Why is nobody listening to anything I say? And, Mom, if you're going to stop by and try to force me to do things I don't want to do, could you at least call beforehand so I have some warning?"

Mom sighed as she headed to the door. "Fine."

Iris half-expected her to add, *This is no way to treat your mother!* But she didn't.

Once Mom and Ngin Ngin were gone, Iris went to her bedroom and collapsed on her bed. She didn't like fighting with her family, but what else could she do when they refused to listen?

She tried to push her family out of her mind and think about tomorrow. She'd never dreaded a conversation with her boss so much, but it was the right thing to do. If she didn't tell him the truth, she'd feel like she didn't have any integrity. What exactly should she say?

Her mind turned to Alex. What was he doing right now? Was he at the gym, building his muscles? Why was she suddenly experiencing a desperate urge to lick his abs?

God, she was such a mess.

15

THE NEXT MORNING, Iris knocked on the door to Scott's office.

"Come in," he said.

She stepped inside and closed the door behind her. Lowry Engineering was too small to have a human resources department, so she had to go to her boss.

"I have to talk to you about something," she said, taking a seat. "It'll only take five minutes, I promise."

He pushed aside the drawings on his desk. "What is it?"

The air-conditioning in the office was on full blast, but she was sweating.

"The East Markham Hospital project," she said. "I… I have developed a personal relationship of sorts with the site supervisor, and I know this is a conflict of interest."

Scott put his elbows on his desk and leaned forward. "Did he harass you? Did he…force himself on you?"

"Oh, God, no. Nothing like that. Anything that happened was consenting." Her cheeks burned. "I am so, so sorry. I don't believe it affected my work at all, but I had to tell you."

His face betrayed no emotion. "Has this been an issue with any other projects you've worked on?"

Iris shook her head vigorously. "No, and I promise it won't happen again."

She felt like crying. She couldn't believe she'd gotten herself into this situation, couldn't believe she'd behaved so foolishly.

She never should have said yes when Alex invited her out for coffee.

"Alright," Scott said. "I think it's best that I reassign the East Markham site visits to Chris. I won't tell him the reason."

"Thank you." Iris twisted her hands together and waited for him to get angry. Was Scott thinking about how this probably wouldn't have happened if he'd hired a male engineer?

But his expression remained impassive.

"You can go now," he said at last.

She drew her eyebrows together, a bit confused by his response. He'd simply accepted it, hadn't even said he was disappointed in her.

She wouldn't question it, though. She left his office and headed back to her desk, where she started organizing the papers strewn about the large surface.

"Is everything okay?" Emma asked. "You just talked to Scott, and now you're cleaning your desk."

Iris managed a small smile. "I'm fine."

Emma stood up. "Come on. Let's take a five-minute break." She pulled Iris outside, and they sat at the picnic table at the back of their office building, where no one else would hear them. "Tell me what's up. I promise I won't tell anyone."

Iris knew she could trust Emma. She just hated to think of her mentor losing respect for her, but the words tumbled out of her mouth anyway.

"The site supervisor on the East Markham project. Alex Kwong. You met him, right?"

Emma nodded.

"We were sleeping together. Actually, it was more than that. I even took him to meet my grandmother. And you're not supposed to be too friendly with the general contractor because you need to be able to take them to task when something isn't going right. I'm sure I could have done my work effectively, and I doubt Alex would say anything to anyone else at work, but if it came out, it would look awful. I couldn't pretend it wasn't happening and wait for everything to blow up." Iris blew out a breath. "Now I feel like I've disappointed every female engineer. Like this reflects badly on all of us."

"You told me you had a one-night stand before you met on site," Emma said, "but more happened after that?"

"Yes."

"Are you still seeing each other?"

"I don't think so."

Emma's eyebrows shot up. "I doubt you would have allowed this to happen unless there was something… Well, I hate to use the word 'special,' but that's what comes to mind. Something special between you two."

Iris snorted. "You're making it sound like we're in love, but we're not. I lack professionalism, that's all."

"You told your boss, even though I'm sure that was an awkward conversation. I don't think most people would have been so forthcoming." Emma paused. "Alex isn't married, is he?"

"No. I never would have done it if he had been."

"What did Scott say?"

"Not much. He just said he'd put Chris on the project." Iris put her head in her hands. "How could I have been so stupid?"

"You're human," Emma said. "I know sometimes it feels like women aren't allowed to be human, like we have to be absolutely perfect to garner as much respect as a barely-competent man, but we *are* human. You do good work, Iris, and Scott is a reasonable person. It'll be okay. We all screw up sometimes."

Iris didn't like Emma saying that she'd screwed up; it pained her to hear someone else speak of her relationship with Alex that way, even if she herself considered it a mistake. A woman would be lucky to have Alex as a boyfriend.

A woman who had any interest in relationships, that was.

It was two o'clock on Tuesday afternoon, and Alex was at the trailer, expecting Iris to show up any minute. She usually came right when she said she would, as though she was never affected by traffic delays. Strangely, however, she'd told her plans to the project manager this time, rather than texting Alex.

Fifteen minutes later, he was about to send Iris a message when an unfamiliar car pulled into the parking lot. A young man stepped out. He put on his safety vest, hardhat, and work boots before heading over to the trailer.

"Hi," he said, extending a hand. "I'm Chris. I'll be taking over from Iris."

"What happened to Iris?" Alex asked.

Chris shrugged. "Not sure. I think she's really busy with another project, so the boss asked me to do this for her."

Alex stared at Chris. Why hadn't Iris told him this was happening? He'd just seen her on Saturday. Or maybe it had happened yesterday or today, but still. Why hadn't she texted him?

What was going on?

Alex called Iris immediately after Chris left. She answered on the first ring.

"Why didn't you come to site today?" he asked. "Is something wrong?"

"Nothing's wrong."

Yeah, right. "Do you want to tell me what's happening?"

"I can't work on this project anymore. Because of you. I told my boss about us. Don't worry, I didn't say much, but I had to explain my conflict of interest."

"I don't understand. Why can't you work on this project?" It wasn't like Alex was her boss.

She sighed. "I'm the engineer on the project. I have to make sure everything is done correctly. If there are any problems, and it comes out that we were sleeping together..." She sighed again. "This is for the best."

"Shit," he muttered. She was right, but it had never occurred to him. However... "Why didn't you tell me? I didn't find out until Chris showed up on site."

That, more than anything, told him there was something wrong between them.

"I don't think we should see each other anymore," Iris said, and her words nearly knocked the wind out of him. "This has screwed up my life enough as it is."

"You're off the project now," he protested when he found his voice. "The damage has already been done."

"I can't. I just can't."

"Explain."

"We're essentially in a relationship, and I never wanted a relationship with anyone. I always wanted to keep my freedom and independence. When I realized the conflict of interest problems, that knocked some sense back into my head. Relationships just cause trouble."

On one hand, he understood. He'd thought that way before, too.

But his mother had told him that one day he'd meet the woman who would change his mind about relationships and marriage.

Some people never wanted those things, and that was fine, but Alex wasn't one of them. And Iris was the woman who'd changed his mind.

He didn't say anything for a moment, too stunned by the realization.

"Come over after work," he said, his voice rough. "We need to talk."

～

Iris drove straight to Alex's apartment after work and parked on the street in front of his building. She took a few deep breaths after turning off the ignition, her hands still gripping the wheel.

He'd asked her to come over, and she hadn't protested. She felt like she owed him this. They'd been close enough that an in-person ending to their relationship was in order.

How the hell had she found herself in this situation?

She got out of the car. Just a quick conversation, and then she'd head home. This would be the last time she saw Alex.

The thought was a punch to her gut.

He'd become an important part of her life in the past few weeks. She didn't want to think about what life would be like without frantic make-out sessions against his front door, lazy mornings cuddled up in bed, burnt scrambled eggs.

She pushed those thoughts aside and marched to his door, head held high.

Her resolve faltered as soon as she saw Alex, his expression serious, his eyes practically burning holes through her. He closed the door behind her, and without saying a word, he wrapped his arms around her and crushed her body against him, his kisses wet and searing.

She could tell him to stop, but she didn't, because God, it felt so good to be in his arms, to revel in how *physical* things could be between them.

But it wasn't just a physical relationship. It was more than that.

"You can't tell me you never want to do that again," he growled, his lips a hair's breadth from hers.

"There are other men out there. It'll be simpler with them. I don't need *you*."

It felt like a lie, but she didn't take it back.

"Fuck, Iris. It wouldn't be like that with anyone else."

"You're really full of yourself, aren't you?"

"You're scared," he said. "You think you're tough. Strong. And you are, but you're also really fucking scared, just because you woke up in my bed the past two Saturdays. That's too much for you."

"What the hell happened to you? The night we met, you just wanted to use me to forget."

He trapped her between his arms, against the door, and God help her, it thrilled her, the pressure of his hard body against hers.

"You happened," he said simply.

Her emotions warred inside her. A part of her couldn't help but be pleased she'd captured this man's attention and affection.

But dammit. She didn't want this.

Why not? a small voice inside her asked.

And then he kissed her again. He kissed her thoroughly, his hands moving all over her body, showing her that no, it really couldn't be like this with anyone else.

Iris had been with many men. She had lots to compare him to.

"You're right," she whispered. "It's different with you."

It had been different since the beginning, if she was honest with herself, but even more so now that they really knew each other. The conversations they'd shared, the comfort they'd offered each other—it mattered. She'd resisted when Emma said he was special, but it was true, much as she loathed to admit it. Alex had snuck in past her defenses somehow; this never would have happened with anyone else.

How could she give this up when it brought her so much pleasure? It was impossible.

There was nothing to do but surrender.

He hurriedly unbuttoned her pants and slipped his fingers inside her.

"Alex," she murmured.

He was on his knees now. He pushed down her pants and underwear and began licking between her legs, running his tongue along her slit, circling her clit.

She thrust her hands into his hair and held him against her as he pleasured her with his mouth. God, he felt so good.

He looked up at her for a moment, his lips glistening with her moisture, and it was so fucking hot. Then he dove between her legs again, giving her exactly what she needed to climax and cry out his name.

Afterward, she slid to the floor, her legs feeling like jelly. He sat beside her.

"You never let a man take care of you, Iris," he murmured, his lips sliding up her neck. "But I'm going to take care of you now."

Gently, he pulled off her pants and underwear and socks, and then he unbuttoned her short-sleeve blouse, kissing her bare skin as it was revealed to him an inch at a time. Her bra was last, followed by his mouth on her breasts. He sucked her nipples, swirled his tongue around them.

She almost melted into the floor.

He scooped her up in his arms and took her to the bedroom. He laid her down on her back, and then he undressed in front of her. Her breath shuddered as more and more of his gorgeous body came into view.

She was used to exploring new bodies when she had sex, but she'd been with Alex several times now, had run her hands all over him. Knew exactly how he reacted when she scraped her fingernails over his back and trailed her hand down his abs to his cock.

She knew him.

And she liked that.

He crawled across the bed until he was on top of her. He kissed her again as his hand slipped between her legs, sliding through her moisture, touching her folds.

"You drive me crazy," he said.

"So do you," she whispered. "So do you."

She could hear the wonder in her voice. How had she gotten to this point with him?

But it didn't matter, not now, because he was touching her and it was bliss.

He watched her face as he stroked her, and she reached between his legs and wrapped her hand around his cock, needing to feel what she did to him. He hissed out a breath. She knew she couldn't touch him for long or he'd come in her hand. Someday, but not now. She needed to feel the pressure of him inside her.

She released her grasp as he slid down her body and licked between her legs again, making her spiral up and up, and then come crashing down in the most marvelous of ways.

She was soft and malleable afterward, and he rolled her onto her stomach and adjusted her so she was on all fours. As he opened the condom packet, she trembled, eager to feel everything he could give her.

He pushed his sheathed cock inside her from behind, ever so slowly, and started to move within her.

She'd never thought of this as a terribly romantic sex position. More like something you did when you wanted it rough and dirty, which was often what she wanted.

But today, with Alex, it was different.

She was consumed by him, and she reveled in it.

Her legs were weak and her knees slid back until she was lying on her stomach, her hips tilted up to allow him entry to her body. He lay on top of her, his chest against her back, and she turned her head to the side so he could kiss her as he moved—deep, satisfying strokes—inside her.

"You're mine," he said, his mouth at her ear.

"Yes," she said in a daze. "Yes."

"I can give you everything you desire."

"Yes."

"You *do* need me."

"Yes."

"I need you, too," he admitted, his lips sliding down to kiss her neck.

He thrust into her harder, and she gasped. He did it again. And again. And then she was crying out, trembling in his arms for a third time, feeling like she was utterly under his spell.

He rolled her onto her back and pushed into her again. He rocked his hips against her as he looked down at her, beads of sweat on his forehead.

When he came inside her, he growled, and she could feel the echo of it in her chest.

She smiled at the pleasure she could give him. It didn't matter what she'd done for other men in the past; all that mattered was that she could please Alex.

He went to the washroom and when he came back a minute later, he lay next to her in bed and ran his hand over her chest, her breasts, her stomach. It wasn't a desperate touch like it had been before. Rather, a gentle, exploring touch.

"You make me feel like I'm alive again," he said.

"Hate to break it to you, but you've been alive this whole time. You're not a zombie."

He playfully bit her shoulder, but his words were serious. "I felt like I'd separated myself from the world. It was necessary, when my mom was very sick and just after she died. I had to keep myself functional, be the person everyone could depend on. But now, with you, I can let myself feel things I couldn't feel before, and it's okay, because you're here with me."

"You're awful mushy."

"It's your fault."

Dimly, she recalled that this wasn't what she'd intended when she'd driven to his apartment after work. She hadn't shown up at the construction site today; she wasn't going to work on the project again because of her conflict of interest. She'd intended to simply have a quick chat with him and then be on her way.

However, she was weak where Alex was concerned.

Maybe it was okay to be with him. They didn't have to make any serious decisions about their future now; they could simply see where this took them.

He pressed kisses down her spine, and she couldn't remember the last time she'd felt this boneless and relaxed. Everything was changing, but it was okay because he was here with her.

She sighed. "I should go home."

"Stay. We'll eat wontons again."

"Ngin Ngin is expecting me for dinner." Though Iris did desperately want to stay with Alex. "You can come, too. She likes you. There's always lots of food in the house. We'll make it work."

"If you're sure she won't mind."

"She won't. Then I'll get my clothes for tomorrow, and we can come back here later."

"I like the sound of that." He kissed her neck, and when he hit a ticklish spot, she giggled.

This was a little surreal. It wasn't like Iris to be snuggled up in bed like this. It wasn't like her to feel like she wasn't in control.

But she couldn't help it, and dammit, she felt good.

It was seven o'clock when Iris skipped up the steps to Ngin Ngin's house and opened the door. Her grandmother would be wondering where she was, ready to serve dinner.

"Hi, Ngin Ngin," Iris said as she slipped off her shoes in the front hall. "Guess who I brought for dinner?"

Strangely, she didn't hear any movement, didn't smell any food cooking.

Her heart beat quickly in her chest. She knew, she just *knew*, that something wasn't right.

"Ngin Ngin?" she called anxiously.

She hurried into the house, Alex behind her.

And there, at the base of the stairs, was her grandmother, lying in a heap on the floor.

16

No.

No, no, no.

Iris crouched on the floor beside her grandmother's twisted body, her heart in her throat. Someone was saying something behind her, but she wasn't paying attention to his words. She was only looking at Ngin Ngin.

Her grandmother's bony hand reached out and encircled Iris's wrist.

"Fell on stairs," Ngin Ngin said, her voice frail. "Much pain… can't move." Her face contorted. "Hurts." She mumbled something else, but the words were unintelligible.

Iris felt like weeping. She wasn't sure whether it was relief that her grandmother was alive and conscious, or sadness that her grandmother was very hurt.

Someone knelt beside her and placed a hand on her shoulder. "I called the ambulance. They'll be here any minute."

Alex. Right.

She couldn't look at him. Her eyes stayed on Ngin Ngin.

"How long ago did you fall?" Iris asked.

"Don't know." Ngin Ngin was silent for a while. "Maybe one hour."

One hour! Thank God it hadn't been longer, but Iris should have been here.

"I'm so sorry," Iris said in a whisper. "So, so sorry."

Ngin Ngin mumbled something in Toisanese, and then there was the wail of sirens outside, and Alex went to the door. A moment later, paramedics rushed in, and Iris felt like she was watching the scene unfold from above. She didn't feel like she was really present. Didn't feel like this was her life, and yet she knew that it was.

A few minutes before midnight, Iris entered the house again, Alex behind her.

They'd spent several hours at the hospital. Ngin Ngin's hip was broken, and her surgery was scheduled for tomorrow morning.

Iris had spent too much time reading about hip fractures on her phone. Many elderly people who broke their hip never regained their independence. The road to recovery would be long. A lot of physical therapy.

And Ngin Ngin was ninety-one years old.

There was a good chance she would never live in this house again. The three steps up to the porch, all the stairs inside, the narrow hallways… It was an old house, not built to accommodate mobility issues.

Her grandmother loved this house, so close to Chinatown and Kensington Market, that she and Yeh Yeh had bought fifty-six years ago, after scrimping and saving for years. She had lots of friends in the area.

She would be heartbroken.

On the way to the hospital, Iris had called her parents, who arrived downtown within half an hour, and Rebecca. Dad had called Uncle Howard, who would come in from Mosquito Bay tomorrow morning.

Mom had finally gotten to meet Alex. How about that.

Alex had stayed the whole time, rubbing her shoulders, bringing everyone coffee and food. He hadn't said much, but he'd been there, a solid presence she could lean on. She'd always thought she would be better in an emergency than she'd been tonight.

As she walked through the house now, her gaze landed on the place at the base of the staircase where her grandmother had been lying, practically motionless, in unbearable pain.

Iris should have been here when it happened. She should have come home right after work. In fact, maybe it wouldn't have even happened if she'd been here. Perhaps Ngin Ngin would have asked her to fetch something from upstairs rather than going herself.

Iris collapsed on the first step of the staircase and put her head in her hands.

Now her grandmother was in the hospital and would probably never get to live in the house she loved again.

"Why didn't you come home until seven o'clock?" Mom had asked her.

"I was…with Alex." Iris had choked out the words, and she'd seen the judgment in her mother's eyes.

She'd moved in with Ngin Ngin almost two months ago; she was supposed to help her aging grandmother around the house. Instead, this had happened.

She sobbed, and Alex sat beside her and put a hand on her back.

"It's my fault," she said.

"No, it's not." He wrapped his arms around her. "I'll stay with you tonight. I need to wake up early to go home and get ready for work, but I can stay the night."

She shook him off. "I can take care of myself."

"I know you can, but let me be here for you."

It was tempting, but she quickly brushed those thoughts aside. "You need to leave," she said.

He frowned. "If you insist, but—"

"You need to leave, and I don't ever want to see you again." She trembled as she said the words, but she meant them. She did.

"Iris, what the hell? You're just in shock because of what happened."

"It's all because of *you*. If I hadn't been with you, I would have heard my grandmother fall, or maybe she wouldn't have even gone upstairs and this whole thing could have been avoided. If it hadn't been for you, I would still be working on the East Markham Hospital job, rather than having to tell my boss that I'd developed a personal relationship with the site supervisor. It was humiliating, and I can't bear to imagine what he thinks of me now." She poked him in the chest with her finger. "It's all because I let myself get involved with *you*, against my better judgment. I don't do relationships, and yet somehow I've found myself in one. All they do is bring pain and stifle your independence. So, no, I don't need to see you again. We're done."

She kept her head held high. She refused to show him how painful those words were for her to say.

Because she *had* grown attached to Alex, against her better judgment.

He shook his head. "No. That's *not* all relationships do, and I confess I never really understood the appeal before I met you. But with you, it's different. Like I said, you make me feel like I'm alive again."

"You said that right after you'd come inside me." She couldn't help being crude.

"That doesn't mean it's not true."

"It means you weren't thinking clearly."

He scrubbed his hand through his hair, clearly frustrated. She hated doing this to him, but it was necessary.

"I love you," he said, anger in his voice. "Don't you dare tell me I'm not thinking clearly now."

She just laughed.

"Why are you laughing? I love you. Do you think you're not lovable? What's so funny?"

She stared at him and shook her head. "I can't believe we've come to this. It was supposed to one fun night of sex, and now it's a fucking mess."

"Maybe it's a bit of a mess, and I wish some things had happened differently, but that doesn't mean it's not real. That doesn't mean we shouldn't be together. There are good times and bad times, and I want to be with you for all of them." There was a bit of wonder in his expression, as though he'd surprised himself by that sentiment, but he didn't take anything back.

"Are you going to propose now?" Iris asked flippantly.

"Don't think about the future. Just let me stay the night and hold you. That's all I ask."

She stood up and pointed toward the front door.

"Leave," she said.

After staring at her for a moment, he nodded and went to the door without a word.

17

IRIS WENT to work on Wednesday, but she wasn't as productive as usual. If she hadn't just told Scott about her conflict of interest, she might have taken the day off because her grandmother was having surgery, but she felt like she couldn't afford to be away from the office. She needed to prove she was a good, dedicated employee.

At lunch, her parents texted to say the surgery had gone fine, and Iris breathed out a sigh of relief.

She didn't go to the hospital after work, not wanting to overwhelm her grandmother with visitors soon after her surgery, but she went on Thursday. Rebecca was already in the room when she arrived.

"You're not allowed to worry about me," Ngin Ngin was saying as Iris entered. "Not good for baby if you worry."

"You can't just tell me not to worry about you," Rebecca said.

"I'm old and sick. Everyone should do what I want."

"Hi, Ngin Ngin." Iris took the seat beside Rebecca. She reached over and squeezed her grandmother's hand. "How are you?"

"I've been better."

Iris managed a smile. "You sound like yourself."

Ngin Ngin's voice was a little fainter than usual, but otherwise, it was true.

"Of course I sound like myself," Ngin Ngin said. "Who else am I supposed to sound like? Justin Trudeau? Can't wait to get out of here."

"You'll need to stay for at least a few days," Rebecca said.

"Aiyah. Iris will blow up my kitchen by then."

Iris chuckled. "I'm really not that bad."

"Make sure you water the herbs in the window box, okay?"

"Okay." Iris paused. "You won't be able to go home right after you get out of the hospital. You may go to a rehabilitation facility for a few weeks, or Mom and Dad said you can live with them. It'll be better for you as you regain your mobility. Their house is more accessible, and there will be more people to look after you. They will arrange any physiotherapy and other appointments you might need."

She wasn't sure if anyone had had this conversation with her grandmother yet, but they needed to start getting Ngin Ngin used to the idea. She couldn't go back to the life she'd had.

It pained Iris to say that to her grandmother, but it was the truth.

"Hmph," Ngin Ngin said. "I don't like this plan."

"Like it or not, you are ninety-one years old and you just broke your hip."

"Living with Carolyn will drive me crazy."

"I know. Living with Mom drives me crazy, too, but they'll take good care of you, okay?"

"I prefer to live with you."

"I can stay with my parents for a little while," Iris said.

"But then you won't live at my house. Who will water my plants?"

"I can come down often enough to water your plants. Or we can get one of your friends in the neighborhood to do it."

"You must call my friends," Ngin Ngin said. "Tell them I'm in hospital. You know where I keep my address book?"

Iris nodded.

"You call Rosetta, Dee, and Mrs. Yee."

"I'll do that."

"You know the last time I stayed in hospital? Very long time ago." Ngin Ngin looked at Rebecca. "When your dad was born. I was so scared. Not knowing what was going on, so much pain. Doctor said mean things. I don't know what he said because I didn't speak English then, but I knew they were mean. I told myself, I must do everything so I never need to stay in hospital again. And I succeeded for more than sixty years. See? I'm stubborn. You tell them, I'm stubborn. I will be able to go back to my house very soon."

On one hand, it seemed good that Ngin Ngin was so positive, but she was in denial of reality, and that wasn't like her. Iris didn't feel like pushing it now, though. Ngin Ngin would still be in the hospital for a little while.

Rebecca gasped.

"What is it?" Ngin Ngin asked. "Is baby coming?"

"No, he's just kicking," Rebecca said. "He's very active."

"Let me feel."

Rebecca waddled over to the bed. She took Ngin Ngin's hand and placed it on her belly.

"I don't feel anything. Maybe he doesn't like me." Ngin Ngin frowned, but then her face brightened. "There. I feel a kick."

Iris felt unequipped to handle all the changes in her life. Her grandmother had just had surgery, her cousin was days away from giving birth. It was too much.

She wished Alex was beside her, but she'd sent him away.

It was necessary. I had to.

"Where's Elliot?" Ngin Ngin asked Rebecca.

"He's at work," Rebecca said, sitting back down. "He should be here soon."

"He will be in the delivery room when you give birth?"

"That's the plan."

"In my day, husbands were not in the room. Probably for the best. Your yeh yeh wouldn't have handled it well." Ngin Ngin turned to Iris. "Where's Alex?"

"At work."

Actually, he'd probably be home by now, but she wouldn't be seeing him today.

"When I'm better, you invite him over. I will cook for him again."

Iris smiled sadly. "Okay, Ngin Ngin. I'll do that."

Alex snagged a booth near the back of The Thirsty Lumberjack and drummed his fingers on the table as he waited for Jamie. He scowled at his beer. The bar didn't have any stouts on tap right now, so he was drinking a pilsner.

It was just like the night he'd met Iris here more than two months ago, except that time he'd been in a bad mood because of his father's unexpected visit with an unnecessary box of food, and now he was in a bad mood because Iris had rejected him.

He'd sent her a few text messages today, the first one asking if her grandmother's surgery had gone okay. Iris had told him that Ngin Ngin was fine, but she hadn't said anything else.

Jamie ambled in and sat across from him. "Weekday night at the bar. Must be serious."

Alex shrugged.

"It's that girl, isn't it?"

He hadn't seen Jamie in a while. His friend had no idea what had happened with Iris in the past two weeks.

"I invited her out for coffee," Alex said, "and then…"

He told Jamie about meeting Iris's grandmother, the two Friday nights and Saturday mornings they'd spent together, and then Tuesday, when Chris had shown up on site instead of Iris. Hard to believe that was only two days ago. He described going to Iris's grandmother's house, the evening spent in the hospital, the fight on the staircase.

Walking down the hallways of the hospital had given him heart palpitations, reminding him of all the times he'd visited his mother at East Markham Hospital as her body withered away. But he'd pushed those thoughts aside and stayed there for Iris.

He'd thought she cared for him, too, but then she'd told him she never wanted to see him again. She was racked with guilt, and he understood. If he were in her shoes, he would have felt the same way, even if logically he knew it wasn't his fault.

"And then," he said with a sigh, "I told her I love her."

Jamie's eyebrows shot up. "Do you?"

"Of course I do. I wouldn't have said it if it wasn't true. Who do you think I am?"

"Okay, okay." Jamie held up his hands, palms out. "Just making sure."

"Anyway, it didn't change anything. She told me to leave."

"Did you sleep at all last night?"

"Maybe an hour. Do I look like complete shit?"

"Yeah, you kind of do."

Alex held up his middle finger, and Jamie laughed.

The waitress came around. Jamie ordered a beer, then slung his arm along the back of the booth once she'd left. "Come on. Pour out all your sappy, melodramatic feelings. I can take it."

"I'm not sure you can," Alex said.

"That bad, eh?"

"How did you get so fucking lucky? You start dating, you fall in love, six months later, you're engaged. Smooth sailing. No problems."

"I wouldn't say there were *no* problems, but compared to what you've been through, I see your point."

"Why did it have to be *her*? She's so stubborn and hot-tempered, and sometimes she just pisses the crap out of me."

Jamie gave him a smile. "And yet you want to kiss her senseless. It could still work out, you know."

"Don't give me false hope."

Alex had thought it himself, of course. He hadn't been able to help himself from looking for hope. Iris had been dealing with a lot when she'd forced him out of the house. Maybe once a few days had passed, she would feel differently. She would realize she loved him, too.

But maybe she didn't feel the same way.

Alex gulped his beer. "Distract me. Tell me something about the wedding. Hell, talk about flowers for twenty minutes, or cake tasting. I don't care."

"It's a bad sign when you're asking me to talk about flower arrangements, not that I could fill even five minutes on flowers. Instead, I'll tell you about some of the ridiculous things my future mother-in-law wants for the ceremony…"

Friday evening, Alex was sitting on the couch in front of the TV, half-watching the Jays game. He was trying—unsuccessfully—not to think about the first time he'd sat on this couch with Iris, when she'd been wearing that gorgeous blue dress. They'd had sex, then eaten rice crackers.

Dammit. He might need to move. Everything in his apartment reminded him of her, and it sucked big time. It felt like she was *everywhere*.

There was a knock at the door, and Alex let out a string of curses. His father. Just what he needed.

Unless it was Iris, and she'd changed her mind…

He hurried to the door and swung it open.

It was his dad, accompanied by a large box of food.

Alex sighed as he ushered his father inside. Hopefully the man would be out of here in five minutes. He really wasn't in the mood for this.

"What was on sale this week?" Alex grumbled. *"Char siu* again?"

"Strawberries." Dad pulled two plastic containers out of the box, followed by a few long eggplants and a package of tofu.

"Great," Alex said, sarcasm edging his voice. "Just what I need."

His dad gave him a look but didn't say anything else as he proceeded to unload the rest of the box. There were cans of water chestnuts and bamboo shoots, a bag of oranges, some lychees, butternut squash, hoisin sauce, cashews, frozen shrimp …

He was getting sick of this.

"Do you like cauliflower?" Dad asked. "You didn't when you were little, but I can't remember if that changed. It was on sale this week, and I wasn't sure whether to buy it for you."

"You do realize I live less than a ten-minute walk from a grocery store, don't you?"

Dad shrugged.

"I can buy my own food. I don't know why you think I'm incapable of doing so."

"I don't," Dad said mildly.

"Then *why*? Because you know who isn't eating? You. Not me. I swear you must have lost at least ten pounds, and you were hardly big to begin with. Maybe you should keep the food for yourself and skip the visit."

Alex knew he shouldn't talk to his father like this, but he couldn't help it. The words just tumbled out of his mouth. He was so pissed off at the world right now, and Iris still wasn't answering his texts.

"You liked it when she did it," Dad said quietly, sitting down at the kitchen table.

"I don't know what you're talking about."

Dad hesitated. "Your mother." He looked guilty as soon as he said the word, as though he wasn't allowed to talk about the woman he'd been married to for thirty-eight years. "She used to drop in unexpectedly and bring you food. Every week or two." His voice wavered. "I was trying to be like her."

Oh.

Alex sat down at the table. His chest felt like it was being clamped in a vise.

"Obviously, I'm not your mother," Dad continued, "but she's not here anymore, and I'm doing the best I can. Because you miss her."

Alex did miss her. So very much. "She would drive halfway across the city to bring me blueberries because they were on sale. I'm sure she used more in gas than she saved on blueberries."

"Yes." Dad smiled faintly. Sadly. "And you'd tell her that, and then you'd bicker, but it was always good-natured. You're different with me. I realized I almost never talked to you without her around, and I don't know how to be with you now that she's gone."

"I realized the same thing."

"It's my fault. I'm your father. Maybe it's partly because I wasn't around enough when you were little. She got pregnant as soon as we moved to Canada, and I was working so hard, trying to be successful in our new country. I didn't spend the time that I should have with you. And now you're all I have here."

Alex swallowed. "Stuart will move back soon."

"I'm glad, but I can hardly bear to think of their baby. It just reminds me of how she isn't here anymore, and she'll never get to see her grandchild."

The air was heavy. It felt like it was compressing his body, weighing him down.

"I think about that, too," he said softly. "Mom would have already bought a box full of things for the baby."

"Yes." Dad paused. "So, I bring you food, because I don't know what else to do. More food than she would because, well, I'm trying to show how much I care."

"Dad," Alex whispered.

"You look good. I mean, aside from the fact that you obviously haven't been sleeping enough, but it looks like you're training for the Olympics."

"Lots of time at the gym, because…"

"I understand," Dad said. "That's just what you do. Whereas I haven't been eating."

"You should really—"

"Some days, I just can't. And to be honest, I don't really know how to cook."

"You don't?"

"She made sure you and Stuart knew what to do in the kitchen before you moved away from home. But not me. She thought she'd always be there to cook for me."

And now she wasn't.

Alex pressed his fingers to the corners of his eyes.

"Sometimes I try to make things," Dad said, "but they taste awful and I have no appetite anyway. Then I bring the ingredients I don't use over to you. That's the other reason I give you so much stuff." He stood up to get a tissue box. "Here." He touched Alex on the back before sitting down.

Tears ran down Alex's face. There had been tears since his mom had died, but very few. He'd kept moving, kept separating himself from his feelings, so this didn't happen.

But it was okay to cry.

It was good to actually talk to his father for once, rather than getting mad at him for bringing over five tins of water chestnuts.

"What about that girl you were seeing?" Dad was probably attempting to cheer Alex up, but it was the wrong thing to say.

"We're not seeing each other anymore. Her choice, not mine."

"Maybe one day…"

His father was probably talking about him meeting another

woman, but Alex hoped that maybe one day, Iris would change her mind. One day.

"I bet Iris is worse in the kitchen than you are," Alex said, managing a smile. "She screwed up scrambled eggs."

"I don't even know how to make scrambled eggs."

"I can teach you."

It was hard to believe this was his life now. Offering to teach his father how to make scrambled eggs.

"You could take cooking classes," Alex said. "Something to do in the evening." *Instead of going home to an empty house.*

"I don't know."

"I could take them with you, if you like."

"Would you?"

Alex nodded. "Yes."

Something for them to do together rather than his father dropping in unexpectedly with too much food once a week. A way to learn to be together, without any other family members around.

"I'd prefer Cantonese cooking," Dad said.

"It's Toronto. I'm sure that won't be too hard to find. We'll try for something in the fall. And, Dad, you don't have to try to be like Mom. You're not her, and that's…" Alex's voice trembled. "That's all right. I can't get my mother back, but I still have my father."

"Okay." Dad's voice trembled, too, on that single word. "Okay."

"I'll make more of an effort as well. I know I haven't been the best son. I don't know what to say to you, and then I end up saying nothing. It's not all your fault." Alex stood up, and hesitantly, he went to his father and put his arms around him. It was new and a little awkward, but they were finally making progress. "You can talk about Mom whenever you want. I get the sense you try not to mention her because you're afraid of upsetting me, but there's a good chance I'm already thinking about her. It's okay,

Dad."

His father shook his head. "It's not okay. I miss her every day. Every hour. I thought if I did the things she used to do for you, you'd miss her a tiny bit less and that would be worth it, but I can never replace her. She was one of a kind."

"She was," Alex agreed, a lump in his throat. "She was."

After they ate scrambled eggs and toast for dinner, followed by strawberries and lychees for dessert, his father left, and Alex lay down on the couch. He didn't even have the energy to turn on the TV. He'd been scraped raw by his conversation with his father, though he was glad they'd finally talked for real.

But now, all of his limbs felt like they were made of lead, and his chest still felt like it was being squeezed between two bricks.

Now, more than ever, he wished he had Iris. He wished he could hold her, feel her fingers moving through his hair, scraping across his skin. Making him feel whole.

Dammit, he missed her.

He loved her.

He loved her so, so much.

18

SATURDAY MORNING, Iris planned to do some cleaning. Some vacuuming, dusting, and laundry. But as she lugged the vacuum out of the closet, she was hit by the silence of the house. After years of living alone, she'd lived with her grandmother for only a short time, but she'd already gotten accustomed to Ngin Ngin always being around.

Plus, Iris hadn't been here the past two Saturday mornings. She'd been in Alex's bed.

Screw it. She'd go to the hospital.

When she opened the front door, ready to head out, there was a vase of roses on the steps. They were the same shade of pink as the ones at A Cup of Stars, and she was certain that was not an accident. She remembered every detail of that afternoon, the exact taste of the crumbly currant scone on her tongue, the exact feel of his lips against her temple.

He probably remembered every detail, too.

So much for not thinking about Alex.

There was a small note tied to one of the roses with a piece of ribbon.

Iris, I'm always here for you if you ever change your mind.

She exhaled unsteadily, and then she brought the flowers inside. She inhaled their delicate fragrance before heading out again.

∿

When Iris arrived at the hospital, a bunch of little old Chinese ladies were tottering out of her grandmother's room as they spoke loudly in Toisanese.

"Iris." Ngin Ngin beamed. "Good timing. Now I don't have to be alone. You have one hour with me, then doctor is coming back to do...I'm not sure."

Iris pulled up a chair and sat down. "How are you feeling today?"

"Am making good progress with walking. Using walker, of course. They say I can get out of here tomorrow."

"That's great."

"Then I will go to the rehab facility for a few weeks before moving in with Lewis and Carolyn." Ngin Ngin paused. "Today is Saturday, right? Why didn't you bring Alex? He's not working today. I want to see him again. Tell him stories about you. Admire muscles."

"Ngin Ngin!"

"Ask him to come see me. He's a good boy. He will come."

Iris massaged her temples. "Alex and I are not seeing each other anymore."

Ngin Ngin frowned. "Why not? You like him, yes?"

"But I never want to get married. I don't even want a relationship, and that's what we had."

"Why you so scared of relationships?"

Iris looked down. "You're happier by yourself, aren't you?"

"Aiyah. Is this the whole reason? Me?"

"It's not the only reason, but when you fell, I wasn't there, and I would have been there if it hadn't been for Alex. When I see people in relationships, I can't help but imagine how much better their lives would be without the other person dragging them down. Relationships cause so many problems."

"Iris, you give me a headache."

"You're happier without Yeh Yeh, aren't you?" Iris pressed.

"I wouldn't say happier."

Iris wasn't surprised her grandmother wouldn't admit it, though it was obviously true.

"But," Ngin Ngin continued, "more freedom and independence—yes."

"I value those things highly."

"Of course. You should." Ngin Ngin paused. "Alex is not like your yeh yeh. He will be a good husband. Support what you like to do. You know, your grandfather was not the man I wanted to marry."

"No?"

Ngin Ngin shook her head. "Did not love him. Not in romantic way. Not like in all those books on my Kindle." She nodded at the e-reader on the table beside her. "He was the man I was supposed to marry, the man my parents chose for me, but I wanted to marry someone else. Man I loved."

Iris's eyes widened. "You had another guy?"

"You think all old people are so proper. We haven't been with anyone but the person we marry, and before we marry, we only have kiss on cheek. Ha!"

"Thank you for putting such wonderful images in my head."

But despite Iris's sarcastic tone, she was curious. Ngin Ngin would sometimes talk about their early years in Canada, but she never, ever talked about China, and she'd never gone back to visit. Iris hadn't heard Ngin Ngin mention her own parents before, and she suddenly realized that she didn't even know if Ngin Ngin had any siblings.

"So why didn't you marry him?" Iris asked.

Ngin Ngin sighed. "My family owned land. We weren't like

dukes and duchesses, but we weren't poor. The Communist Party, led by Mao Zedong—you know who he is?"

Iris nodded.

"They started land reforms. You can use the computer to look it up. I don't want to explain all the details, but many landlords were killed. Mao encouraged peasants to kill them."

Iris put a hand to her mouth. She almost told Ngin Ngin to stop, but that wouldn't change what had happened.

"The man you loved…he died?"

Ngin Ngin shook her head. "No. They killed my parents."

Iris was too horrified to speak.

"So I ran to your yeh yeh. I wanted to honor my parents' wishes, but also, he always talked of taking me to Canada. He had an uncle here. I wasn't so sure about going to Canada before, but after they killed my parents, I wanted to escape. Very afraid. Other man wanted to stay in China. I loved him, but I could not stay. So I married your grandfather. We went to Hong Kong and saved money to fly to Vancouver. Then we took the train across Canada. Big country, took long time. We ate only bread and strawberry jam because we didn't know English and could not ask for anything else. But I was excited. I had chance for a new life. Make family proud. It was not perfect choice, but it was the best choice. I still think so. Because look at the life children and grandchildren have! You can do anything you want. You have a good job, opportunities. You don't have to make a decision like me. No reason you cannot be with the man you love."

"I don't love Alex," Iris said faintly, trying to process everything she'd just been told.

"Ah, you're lying. Or you don't know it yet. But I'm an old woman. Very wise. I know."

"What happened to the other man?"

"We wrote each other letters, but then Yeh Yeh found out and got mad. Eventually, my cousin told me he died. Many, many years ago now. Part of the reason Yeh Yeh didn't give me much freedom was punishment for the letters, plus he was afraid I would have an affair since I didn't love him."

Iris clasped her grandmother's hands. "I'm so sorry you had to go through all that." She paused. "Did you have any siblings?"

"I had a brother. He was killed, too."

Iris shut her eyes. "I'm sorry. We don't have to talk about this if you don't want."

"It's okay. You should know these things now."

"Do Dad and Uncle Howard know what you just told me?"

"Not about the other man, but yes. I didn't tell them when they were children, though. You remember you had a family tree project in school? I think you were in grade three."

"Yes. We had to make a family tree, going back to our great-grandparents."

"Your dad called me because he didn't know anything about his grandparents. I didn't want to tell him anything, but eventually I gave dates. Of course, he asked why my parents died on the same day. Very suspicious, yes? So, finally, I told him, but I asked him to lie to you, give you different dates for their deaths. Because you were smart cookie, and I was afraid you'd ask questions. You were eight years old. Too young for that."

Iris squeezed her grandmother's hands. "I don't know what to say."

"You must take advantage of all opportunities. That's why we came here—to give children and grandchildren a better life. You can have everything. Job, husband you love, children, hobbies. So proud of you, Iris."

A tear slid down Iris's cheek as she smiled at her grandmother.

"Thank you," she said. "I wish you'd had all the opportunities I have."

"I would have been a great engineer, don't you think? I would love to boss men around at construction sites."

"You know, that's really not what my job is like."

Ngin Ngin waved her hand. "Close enough. I wonder what my family would think of my life now. I have two granddaughters married to white men. One has PhD and studies climate change; other is going to have a baby any minute. I have a grandson who is married to another man, and they adopted a little girl. I also have a granddaughter who is an engineer and more stubborn than I am. I speak English and have friends from all over the world. I can make tiramisu and pad Thai. They could never imagine this, I don't think."

"You're only ninety-one. You still have time to do more."

"Goal is to live to one hundred. Then if I meet a woman who is ninety-one, I can call her a spring chicken!"

Iris managed a laugh, though there were still tears in her eyes.

"Now I'm tired," Ngin Ngin said. "Want to rest before doctor comes. You can leave. Go find Alex. Maybe he's at the gym, making all those muscles, or maybe he's writing you a romantic letter? I don't know. You go find him, and soon you bring him to visit me."

"Actually, I'm visiting my parents this afternoon." They were supposed to talk about how to re-arrange the house so Ngin Ngin could move in when she got out of the rehab facility, but Iris didn't feel like mentioning that, not now.

"Okay. Eventually you will realize I'm right."

"Maybe I will."

Before returning to Ngin Ngin's house, Iris went to a coffee shop near the hospital, ordered a latte, and stared blankly out the window.

She was still trying to wrap her mind around everything her grandmother had told her. Her skin felt cold as she thought of her grandmother's past. She'd known almost nothing of her family history—on both sides—before they came to Canada, and she didn't know much of China's history, either.

She'd never been to China, nor had her father. Both her mother and father had been born in Canada, and their families were from the Sze Yup area, the Four Counties, in southern China.

Alex's parents, on the other hand, had grown up in Hong Kong. Alex had been there several times; they'd talked about it once, during one of the mornings Iris had spent curled up in his bed. Now, she imagined going to Hong Kong with him and meeting his extended family.

Alex had started appearing in her plans for the future, whereas before, she'd always imagined herself being alone. She'd liked it that way, but now, she wasn't so sure.

Iris plodded up the walkway to her parents' house in Scarborough. It was the house she'd grown up in, and the area was very Chinese, but now she couldn't help thinking that most families here had quite different histories from her own. None of her childhood friends had parents who'd been born here; none of them had families who'd been in Canada as long as hers.

She'd said she would come around three o'clock, but after drinking her latte and eating a sandwich for lunch, she'd had nothing to do but stare at the pink roses from Alex, so she'd driven here a little early.

She used her key to open the door and stepped inside. She didn't hear any noise, which was odd, and when she glanced in the living room...

What the hell were her parents doing? Her father was sitting sideways on the couch, and her mother was straddling him, her face pressed against his. Her shirt matched her skin tone and...

Oh.

Iris had been wrong about the shirt. Her mother wasn't wearing a goddamn shirt.

Oh, God. No.

At that moment, her father looked up and saw her standing by the French doors. She ran into the kitchen and started frantically looking through the cupboards, needing something to do. She found a package of cookies and stuffed one into her mouth, as though it could wipe the image she'd just seen from her brain, but of course it couldn't.

When her mother walked in a few minutes later, Iris was sitting at the kitchen table, drinking a cup of tea, which wasn't enough to soothe her. Not even the strongest chamomile tea could do much at this point.

Mom sat down across from her. "We weren't actually—"

"You were about two seconds away from doing it!" Iris pressed her palms to her eyes. "Do you have any bleach for my brain? Please?"

"It's perfectly natural—"

"Mom! Can we stop talking about this? Now?"

Mom chuckled. "I don't think your father will be able to look you in the eye today."

"I don't think I can look him in the eye, either. Or you." Iris's hands were still over her eyes. "Strangely, you don't seem bothered by this."

"Why would I be? Like I said, it's perfectly natural—"

"Please don't say that again."

"—and it's not like you really *saw* anything. Besides, you're twenty-seven. You know how these things work. You know we had to do that to make you in the first place."

"Vaguely knowing it and actually seeing it are two different things."

"You should be glad your parents still love each other."

"Oh, dear God." But then Iris thought about it. Her mother's words, not what she'd witnessed in the living room. "You do?

Love each other?"

"Of course. Many people stay married even though they don't love each other, but I would never do that. I'd be single and screwing hot men with tattoos, like you did."

"I don't know why I'm still participating in this conversation," Iris muttered, but that was just for show. She did know.

There had been much more to her grandmother's life than she'd realized, and maybe that was true for her mother, too.

"Sorry if I was judgmental when I found you eating breakfast with a guy," Mom said. "I was just a little surprised. You're my daughter. My little girl. My—"

"Miracle baby. Yeah. I know."

"You were such a fussy baby, but I didn't care. I was just so happy we'd finally managed to have a baby. Though I hope, for Rebecca's sake, that her child is better behaved."

"Thanks, Mom."

"So when I found you that morning, it was hard for me to wrap my head around. Like it was for you today. But when I was young, I was like you."

Yeah, Iris knew her mother had been a bit of a party girl. She'd embraced the drug culture of the seventies and had been determined that her daughter would not do the same.

"You used to tell me stories about when you were young," Iris said. "All the fun you had. All your travels. I loved those stories. I couldn't understand why you married Dad and moved to suburbia and had a boring life."

"You know why I used to do what I did? Because I was miserable. I was always looking for some kind of quick fix. Some kind of escape. Then I met your father, and I didn't feel the need to escape anymore."

Iris frowned. "You do ninety-eight percent of the talking, and whenever he talks, you're usually arguing with each other. And you're *never* affectionate."

Mom gave her a look. "I think we proved otherwise today."

Iris groaned in agony. "Please don't remind me."

"I won't deny that it was tough when we struggled to have a baby. We had planned to have three kids, but then it took us three years to conceive."

"I thought it took you seven?"

"The first time was after we'd been married three years. I was thrilled, but that lasted all of two weeks. I miscarried early on."

"You never told me."

Mom shrugged. "I don't like to think about it. Your father and I had some problems after that, but eventually I realized that even if we couldn't have a kid, it would be okay. We had each other, and that wasn't what we'd dreamed of, but we could make it work. Then you came along." She paused. "Iris, you can't really know what another person's relationship is like from the outside. Ours is good. Trust me."

"You never regret it?"

"Of course not."

"You never wish you could have the life you lived before? The independence of it?"

Mom shook her head. "I miss dancing and I wish your father would agree to take ballroom dancing lessons, but that's about it. I've been asking for three decades and it has yet to happen. But otherwise? I don't know what there is to miss. It's not like getting married took away all my freedom, like you seem to fear. There are lots of things I could still do—other than sleeping around—but I don't do them because I don't want to. Your life doesn't have to completely change because you get married, and if a man doesn't give you the freedom you need, then he's not worth marrying."

Iris had a sip of her tea. "I thought you were setting me up with men just because you saw marriage as a milestone I needed to reach."

"No. I'm happier married, and I thought you might be, too,

but maybe you weren't meeting the right guys by going out to bars and clubs and whatever else you do in your spare time."

"I wasn't miserable, though. Not like you. I was happy with my life."

"And now?"

Iris couldn't help thinking about a certain man. Before, she'd focused on the problems that had resulted from their relationship, like the conflict of interest at work. Now, she could admit that he made her feel like no one else.

She'd been happy enough before, but life was better with him. Sure, it hadn't all gone smoothly. But instead of holding her back, which was what she'd once feared would happen in a relationship, he helped her enjoy the quiet moments in life, and he supported her—like when Ngin Ngin had broken her hip—in a way she'd never experienced with a man before.

She missed him terribly.

"Please stop trying to set me up with men," she told her mother.

"Of course. I met Alex, and clearly he's your boyfriend, even if you refuse to put a label on it. I admit I was doubtful when your grandmother mentioned him, and I was also jealous you'd introduced him to her rather than me first, but I like him. He seems good for you, though I only saw him at the hospital."

"But you said you can't really know what another person's relationship is like."

"I'm your mother. I can tell."

Iris swirled the tea in her cup. "You're not angry that I was at Alex's when Ngin Ngin fell? You seemed upset about that before."

"I wasn't angry at you. Sorry if it seemed that way—I was just in shock. I'm glad you decided to live with her rather than us, even though I didn't feel that way at first. If it hadn't been for you, I don't know when we would have found her, if she would have managed to drag herself to a phone eventually? I don't want to think about it. We gave her that emergency alert bracelet and told her to wear it *all the time*, but she wasn't wearing it when she fell." Mom shook her head. "Silly woman. So stubborn."

"I don't think she's fully accepted that she can't go home when she gets out of the hospital tomorrow. Where will she stay when she lives here?"

Mom stood up, and Iris followed her into the living room. She winced when she saw the couch where her parents had been making out earlier.

"This room is best because it's on the first floor," Mom said. "No stairs. We talked about replacing the French doors, but for now, we'll just put heavy curtains over them. That should be good enough. We'll bring her bed and dresser from her house, so it can be as similar to home as possible, and move the couch upstairs."

"You're going to have your mother-in-law living with you. Are you sure you don't regret marrying Dad? She's going to drive you nuts."

"Stop trying to get me to say I regret it! I don't. Yes, your grandmother and I will drive each other bonkers, but I do care for her."

They said nothing for a little while, and it was strange, being in the same room as her mother and not speaking. They didn't do silence well when they were together.

"Can I ask you something?" Iris asked at last, then continued after her mother nodded. "I know it was before you and Dad met, but why didn't he go to Uncle Howard's wedding? Did he not approve of his brother marrying a white woman?" That had always bothered her.

"Your grandfather declared that no one in the family would go to the wedding, and so your father, wanting to stay on his parents' good side, did not attend. He feels bad about it."

"If I married a white man—"

"Your father would be happy for you, don't you worry, but that's not relevant now, is it? You have Alex, and he's Chinese."

"I don't *have* Alex. I haven't seen him since the night at the hospital."

"You'll figure it out."

"Mom, I…" Iris trailed off when her phone beeped. She checked the message.

It was a picture of a baby boy, eyes closed, pressed against Rebecca's chest.

The next morning, Iris and Crystal grabbed a coffee before they went to visit Rebecca and her new baby at the hospital. It wasn't the same hospital Ngin Ngin would be released from later that day, but nearby.

"I'm meeting Jared's parents tonight," Crystal said as they sat down at a table by the window with their drinks. "I'm so nervous. I've never met a boyfriend's parents before. God, what if I say something really stupid?"

"Listen to you," Iris said. "Talking about your boyfriend."

"I know. Who would have thought? I can't believe we both met men on the same night."

Iris looked down. She didn't protest and say Alex didn't really count, they'd only had sex a few times. That would obviously be a lie.

"I haven't talked to Alex since Tuesday, although when I found out Rebecca had her baby, I couldn't help myself from sending him a text. He's the person I want to tell about everything, you know?"

"I know," Crystal said, placing her hand over Iris's. "Same for me and Jared."

"What the hell happened to us? I thought we were going to stay cool and single and now…"

"We're no less awesome because we have boyfriends who appreciate how awesome we are. Things change, and that's okay.

Even though I break out in a cold sweat whenever I think about tonight, my life has changed for the better. It turns out that I actually like being in a relationship, and not just because of all the sex. A few months ago, I never would have imagined myself saying this, but Iris, I think you need to let Alex be a part of your life. He's not going to turn you into something you're not."

Iris nodded. "I talked to my grandmother and mother, and I realized I never knew the full story of either of their marriages. I started to see that all the reasons I had for avoiding relationships were actually pretty flimsy. They were based on me not under-standing certain things about my family. And myself. I'd also refused to let myself think about how good it felt to be with him —and not just when we were having sex."

"So after we visit Rebecca, you'll run to his door and throw yourself into his arms?"

"I don't know. I only started thinking about it yesterday. I still haven't fully wrapped my mind around the idea. But maybe. Probably."

There. She'd admitted it.

Coffees finished, they headed up to the hospital room. They entered quietly, in case the baby was sleeping. Indeed, he was curled up in Rebecca's arms with his eyes closed, his fist under his chin. Elliot was sitting on the chair beside them.

"How was your first night?" Crystal asked, her voice hushed.

"Not much sleep." Rebecca glanced up, then looked down at the bundle in her arms with a smile. "But that's to be expected."

Iris stepped closer and peered at her cousin's new baby. "He's so cute."

He was rather squished up and funny looking, but definitely still cute.

They stood in silence for a moment, looking at the baby. As if realizing he had four sets of eyes on him, he started squirming and briefly opened his eyes.

"Hi, baby," Rebecca said in a sing-song voice. "Crystal and Iris are here to meet you. Would you like to say hello?" She passed the swaddled baby over to Iris, who took him carefully.

She'd held babies before, but never a newborn. Never a baby that was less than a day old. She was afraid she would screw it up —she'd done that with a bunch of things lately—but the baby seemed content in her arms.

"Does he have a name?" Iris asked.

Rebecca shook her head. "We have some ideas, but we haven't decided yet."

"Your mom's been here already?"

"Last night. Elliot's mother should be here soon."

Iris sat down on the edge of the bed with the baby in her arms. He looked like he was taking his new world very seriously, even though his vision would be limited and he wouldn't be able to see much of it. But he would grow quickly. Soon he would smile, support his head, and roll over.

She glanced up at Rebecca and Elliot. Elliot had his hand on his wife's knee. They looked tired, but they were smiling.

Iris turned back to the baby and started sobbing.

She loved this new baby, and she loved seeing her cousin happy with her husband, and Crystal happy with Jared, and God, she was just so full of love right now.

She loved Alex, too.

Did she want this one day? Sitting in a hospital room with her new baby?

She wasn't sure whether she wanted kids. Frankly, she'd never given it much thought before—it hadn't fit into her vision of her life—but suddenly, it was a possibility.

But whether she decided she wanted a baby like Rebecca or would prefer to remain childless like Natalie, she knew she wanted to be with Alex.

Sure, she still wanted to go out drinking and dancing with Crystal, but more than that, she wanted lazy Saturday mornings in bed with the man she loved. Ordinary weekday dinners that were made special just because she was with him.

She hadn't been a hundred percent sure before, but now, she knew.

She just knew.

In the past, she'd thought it was lame when people said that, but now she understood what they meant.

Rebecca took her son back from Iris and handed her a tissue.

"Have I done more crying than the baby?" Iris asked, sniffling.

"Oh, no. He's quiet now, but he still has you beat by a mile." Rebecca looked down at the baby. "Iris is the sensitive one," she told him. "She cries at all the sad scenes in movies."

"Don't listen to your mother. She has it all wrong."

Crystal and Rebecca laughed. Nobody said anything more for a few minutes, but Rebecca nodded knowingly at Iris.

"Let's take a few pictures," Iris said.

She took one of Rebecca, Elliot, and their son, and then a few close-up shots of the baby. A few tears continued to fall silently down her cheeks, and she had a strange feeling in her chest, like it wasn't big enough to contain her heart.

To be honest, there had been times in Iris's life when she hadn't even been sure she had a heart, but she did.

Oh, she definitely did.

There were many things she wouldn't have known about herself if it hadn't been for Alex, and there were so many things she had yet to learn about herself—and him.

She couldn't wait to start.

19

MEET *me at A Cup of Stars as soon as you can.*

Alex read the text message a second time. It still said the same thing. It wasn't his imagination.

Iris wanted to see him.

He'd been about to go to the gym, but now he tossed aside his gym bag and looked for some nicer clothes. Seeing as he worked on a construction site, he didn't exactly wear nice clothes to work, but he still had a few dress shirts. He put one on, as well as a pair of khakis, and half-jogged to the coffee shop.

He didn't see her inside, but he hadn't expected to.

She was exactly where he'd thought she would be. On the swinging bench in the backyard patio, wearing the midnight-blue dress she'd worn the night he'd met her.

As he walked over to her, images from the past couple months flashed through his mind. The day she'd shown up on site in her hardhat and safety vest, and they'd argued non-stop. Their coffee date, when he told her about his mother. Dinner at her grand-mother's. The smell of burning eggs. Eating wonton soup together at his kitchen table. Relaxing right here, beneath the murals of flowers and stars.

He'd brought her to A Cup of Stars on a whim. This place was an escape, of sorts, for him; a place where he'd still been able to find a few minutes of peace, even when his mom was dying. He'd always come here alone.

But it had felt right to bring Iris here last Saturday. He'd had the passing thought before that it was a romantic spot, even though he'd almost never thought about romance until recently.

It felt right to be here with her now.

"Iris," he said, sitting down beside her.

"Um." She twisted her hands together. "Hi."

She let him take her hands, and they both looked down at their intertwined fingers.

"You don't need to be nervous," he said. "You got the flowers yesterday, didn't you? I meant what I said in the note." He glanced at the roses on the trellis before turning back to her.

She nodded, then began to speak. "I used to think I would always be alone. Not because I believed no one would ever want me, but because I *wanted* to be alone. I listened to my mother's exciting stories of her single life, and her life with my father sounded dreary in comparison. I saw my grandmother's life improve after her husband died. Once I started getting interested in boys… Well, none of them gave me a reason to change my mind. Until I met you."

Until I met you.

That was how it had been for him, too. Perhaps he hadn't sworn off relationships the way Iris had, but he'd never desired more than a casual fling.

"I'm sorry I freaked out on you on Tuesday," she continued. "You told me you loved me, and I told you to get out. I was frightened. I kept thinking about how I would have been there when my grandmother fell if I hadn't been with you, but maybe I wouldn't have been home anyway. I was focusing only on that—and the issues at work—and I couldn't see how much you've given me in the short time we've known each other. Rather than giving up a part of myself, I found a part of myself when I was with you. Now, I see it so clearly, and I understand my grandmother and my mother's choices, too. Anyway." She took a deep breath. "I don't know if I'm doing a terrible job of this. I've never made a declaration of love before; I've never wanted to. But I love you, Alex, and I'm not going to run away from you again." She wrapped her arms around him, and they held each other in silence for a moment.

He breathed her in. A light, flowery essence that somehow captured her beauty and strength. She felt so wonderful in his arms, and he felt so lucky that he would get to hold her again and again.

"I love you, too," he whispered. "Whether you're threatening to give me amnesia or trying to burn down my kitchen."

"Hey! That only happened because you distracted me with your hot body and talented mouth. And I only wanted to remove twenty-four hours of your memory, nothing more."

"I'm glad you don't have the power to do that, because I quite enjoy those memories of the first time I brought you home with me. Even if I woke up alone the next morning."

"I do apologize for that." She tilted her head back to look up into his eyes. "From now on, I want you to wake up beside me as often as possible."

"Sounds good to me," he said, his voice a little rough.

She kissed his lips—a gentle, lingering kiss—before nodding at the table beside the bench swing. There were two cups of coffee and a plate piled with baked goods, including a currant scone.

Like the time they'd been here a week ago, he broke off a piece of scone and fed it to her, and then she fed him a piece of brownie. The sweets were delicious, especially under the winking stars in the night sky and the giant sunflowers. It was magical here.

The sweets were particularly delicious because he was sharing them with Iris.

But he wasn't in the mood for a leisurely coffee date today, not when he wanted to tear off her blue dress. They both finished their coffees quickly and hurried back to his apartment, where he pressed her against the door and kissed her senseless. They finally made it to the bedroom, and when he slid inside her, it took his breath away.

She was just what he wanted.

∼

A little while later, Alex woke up to find Iris climbing back into bed.

"I was hungry again," she said, "so I made a snack."

"Did you turn on the stove? Does the rest of my apartment still exist?"

She cuffed him on the shoulder, then made a very thorough exploration of his biceps and chest before she returned her attention to the plate in front of her.

"Last time I checked," she said, "cheese and crackers don't require any cooking."

He helped himself to a piece of cheese. "My father and I are going to take Cantonese cooking classes at the cultural center. Maybe you could join us? Actually, I should probably check that my father would be okay with that. I should also check that the place has a good sprinkler system installed."

"I'm not that bad!"

"I know."

"A single fire extinguisher would probably be enough to deal with my mistakes, but perhaps it wouldn't make the best impression on your father if we got to know each other in a kitchen. Just keep it as time for the two of you. Though I would like to meet him. Soon."

He pulled her closer. "My father came over unexpectedly with another box of food on Wednesday, and we talked. He said he was trying to do the things that my mother used to do for me." Alex released a shuddering breath. The thought that Iris would never get to meet his mother was hard to bear. "But she's gone, and Dad and I have to learn to be together when it's just the two of us."

Iris plucked a cracker and a piece of cheese from the plate before leaning back against him. "You'll figure it out. I have faith in you."

He smiled against her neck before kissing her.

She was here with him, and everything was okay.

When Iris and Alex arrived at Rebecca's apartment the following Saturday, everyone else was already there. She hoped he didn't find her family overwhelming.

"This is Rebecca, Elliot, and little Nicholas," she said as they approached the couch. Nicholas wailed in response. "This is Natalie, Rebecca's older sister. You've met Ngin Ngin and my parents before." Her parents had driven Ngin Ngin from the rehab facility, where she had already made several new friends, to visit her new great-grandson.

Alex nodded and said hello to them all before he and Iris sat down on the loveseat.

"You see?" Ngin Ngin said. "Now my work is done. All four grandchildren married—"

"Married!" Mom's head snapped toward Ngin Ngin. "Do you know something I don't know? Iris, did you secretly tie the knot? Why wasn't I invited? You're my only child!"

Ngin Ngin laughed. "Ah, Carolyn, I just said that to see if you'd notice. As far as I know, Iris isn't married." She looked at Iris for confirmation.

"Not married," Iris confirmed, but one day, she knew she'd be married to the man sitting next to her. Not long ago, she would have recoiled at such a thought, but now, everything was different.

She took Alex's hand and squeezed it.

"It's okay," Ngin Ngin said. "At least you're no longer saying he's not your boyfriend. Good enough for me. You can wait to get married, but not too long because I'm getting old. Maybe you can have a baby, too, but if you don't want babies, it's okay. Already have Nicholas."

At that comment, Nicholas wailed again.

"Pass him to me," Ngin Ngin said, and Elliot stood up and handed her the baby. "Lucky to live to have great-grandson, even if I busted my hip. And look! He stopped fussing. I have the magic touch."

"You sure do," Mom said.

Dad was sitting on the chair beside her, and he made an inarticulate grunt, which usually meant "yes." Iris now found herself looking at her parents' lives from a different perspective. Unfortunately, her father was still unable to make eye contact with her after the events of last Saturday afternoon.

Too bad nobody had invented brain bleach yet.

"How did you and Alex meet?" Natalie asked.

"Oh." Iris felt herself blushing. "We met at a bar, and then we were kind of working on a project together, and...it's complicated."

Their path here might have been a little complicated, but everything seemed simple now.

They loved each other.

She was lucky she wasn't like her grandmother, who'd had to choose between the man she loved and the man who would take her to Canada to start a new life.

Iris could have it all.

"Alex," Ngin Ngin said. "Take the baby from me, now that I've calmed him."

Alex dutifully got up and accepted the little bundle. He sat back down beside Iris, and Nicholas appeared to regard him thoughtfully.

And, okay, Iris did get a warm, mushy feeling when she saw Alex holding a baby and smiling. She couldn't help it.

Maybe they would have one eventually. Her mother was probably desperate to have a grandchild to fuss over and would start bugging Iris about it soon. Not that she'd ever listened to what her mother told her to do.

But although Iris didn't know where life would take her, she did know one thing.

She and Alex would be together.

[EPILOGUE]

Several months later...

It was the final afternoon of work before the holidays. Lowry Engineering would be closed for more than a week, until January.

Well, saying it was an afternoon of work was really stretching the definition of the word, since they were having a party.

Iris popped a chocolate in her mouth, then turned to Emma. "What are your plans for the holidays?"

"We have to do Christmas three times in three days, and two of those are out of town. I just hope nobody gets sick, because I don't need a repeat of last year." Emma sighed dramatically. "I'm going to get more egg nog. Want some?"

Iris shook her head.

Emma walked away in search of egg nog, and Scott appeared beside Iris.

"I got your save-the-date email," he said.

Iris smiled. "Yes, I'm getting married in June." She was inviting Scott, Emma, and one other engineer in the office.

"Which surprised me. I hadn't known you were seeing anyone." He looked at her hands. "Ah. You're wearing a ring."

"I've been wearing it for two months." She paused. "You actually *did* know I was seeing someone."

He raised his eyebrows. "Really?"

"Remember my conflict of interest for the East Markham Hospital project? The site supervisor?" When he nodded, she continued. "Why weren't you angrier at me for that?"

"I knew it was a one-off. You were so embarrassed and ashamed that I was sure it would never happen again."

"It won't. Because I'm marrying him." She wasn't ashamed of what had happened, not anymore. It wouldn't have happened with anyone but Alex.

"So I see. Congratulations."

"Thank you."

He headed off in the direction of the food, and Emma returned. "So, what are you doing for the holidays, Iris? Lots of wedding planning?"

When Iris arrived home, the house smelled amazing.

Alex had moved into Ngin Ngin's house with Iris after they'd gotten engaged, and last weekend, they'd put up a Christmas tree, which smelled lovely.

But it wasn't just the Christmas tree.

"Are you baking?" she called out as she took off her boots.

Alex appeared in front of her with a plate of shortbread cookies, and she couldn't help but grin.

"Is that smile for me or the cookies?" he asked, placing a kiss on her cheek.

"You, of course," she said, but she plucked a cookie from the plate, even though she'd already eaten her weight in sugar today.

The cookie was better than anything she could have baked herself, that was for sure.

He led her to the ugly brown couch, and she snuggled up against him.

She did, indeed, like her new life very much, but she didn't regret the way she'd lived before: lots of going out, one-night stands. She'd enjoyed it at the time, and it had led her to Alex.

It was a very good thing that she and Crystal had gone to The Thirsty Lumberjack that night in their quest to find men. Iris had met Alex, and Crystal had met Jared—and they were getting married, too. Next fall. Iris would be a bridesmaid.

This was her first Christmas in a relationship. In addition to seeing her family on Christmas Day, she would be joining Alex's family on Christmas Eve at his father's house. His brother and sister-in-law had moved to Toronto a few months ago, and Ericka was now nearly nine months pregnant. Iris had bet Alex that the baby would be born in December; Alex was convinced she wouldn't make an appearance until the New Year. Whoever lost had to make the other person a romantic dinner.

Hmm. Perhaps Alex actually wanted to lose so Iris wouldn't set fire to anything.

She reached for another shortbread cookie—a star decorated with sprinkles—and looked around the cozy house. She loved coming home to her fiancé. Loved going to sleep next to him and waking up next to him.

So much had changed this year, and she couldn't wait to see what the New Year would bring. Rebecca and Nicholas were doing well. Ngin Ngin had regained most of her mobility, but had agreed to remain with Iris's parents in Scarborough for now, though she visited Iris and Alex at her house every week.

This spring, Alex planned to turn the tiny patch of grass in the backyard into a garden, complete with a swinging bench and roses. Perhaps some peonies, too.

By late summer, Nicholas would be walking, and Iris and Alex would be married.

Married.

She'd never wanted that for herself before, but thanks to the man sitting next to her, she'd changed her mind.

Alex pressed his forehead to hers, his breath warm on her face, and kissed her.

This would be the best Christmas ever.

Because she'd be spending it with the man she loved.

ACKNOWLEDGMENTS

Thank you to Rain Merton for their help with the manuscript, and to my editor, Latoya C. Smith, for helping me make this book the best it could be. Thank you also to Toronto Romance Writers, as well as my husband and father, for all your support. Lastly, thank you to Flirtation Designs for the lovely cover!

Jackie Lau decided she wanted to be a writer when she was in grade two, sometime between writing "The Heart That Got Lost" and "The Land of Shapes." She later studied engineering and worked as a geophysicist before turning to writing romance novels. Jackie lives in Toronto with her husband, and despite living in Canada her whole life, she hates winter. When she's not writing, she enjoys gelato, gourmet donuts, cooking, hiking, and reading on the balcony when it's raining.

To learn more and sign up for her newsletter, visit
jackielaubooks.com.

DISCARD

CPSIA information can be obtained
at www.ICGtesting.com
Printed in the USA
BVHW032146061119
563147BV00001B/10/P